THE BRIDEGROOM WAS A DOG

THE BRIDEGROOM WAS A DOG

Yoko Tawada

Translated by
Margaret Mitsutani

KODANSHA INTERNATIONAL
Tokyo • New York • London

Publication of this translation was assisted by a grant from the Japan Foundation.

Line drawings by Ryuji Watanabe.

The Japanese titles of these stories are, consecutively: *Inumukoiri* (1993), *Kakato o nakushite* (1992), and *Gotthard tetsudo* (1996). All were originally published by Kodansha Ltd.

First edition, 1998
ISBN 4-7700-2307-3
98 99 00 01 02 10 9 8 7 6 5 4 3 2 1

THE BRIDEGROOM
WAS A DOG

$\mathcal{T}$he mid-afternoon sunlight stuck, pure white, to the vertical and horizontal washing on the lines as an old man, walking through a large apartment complex in the airless, clammy heat, suddenly stopped in the middle of the road to look back over his shoulder and froze that way, and a brick-red car ground to a halt beside a mailbox as if its strength had petered out, though no one got out into the stillness of a July day at two o'clock, silent except for a distant drone that might have been either a dying mosquito or the hum of a machine in a school-lunch factory.

In a six-mat room beyond the railing on her balcony a housewife was making tea, stopping now and then to frown at the blank TV screen as she picked at a scab on her knee; her neighbor, who had gone to the local Culture Center, had closed her kitchen curtains but not all the way, so you could see a half-eaten apple with lipstick stains on top of the refrigerator. In one corner of this apartment complex in a modern residential area, so dull it seemed dead until the children came home to get ready for cram school, there was a large, dirty, home-made sign that had been clinging to a telephone pole for a year or more, always seeming about to fall off but somehow stubbornly managing to stay on. The rain had blurred the words "Kitamura School," written with a pink magic marker in Mitsuko Kitamura's handwriting, and the telephone number was half torn off, and there was so much yellow pigeon shit stuck to the map you could hardly read it, but since all the mothers in the complex with children of elementary or junior high school age knew where the Kitamura School was this didn't pose a problem, and although the poster had out-lived its usefulness no one bothered to dispose of it, either because it was too filthy to touch, or out of loy-alty to the tradition, firmly established in the thirty years since the complex had been built, of not worrying about how dirty things outside were as long as the area around your own apartment was clean, which meant that when a pigeon was hit by a car and lay splattered all over the street or some drunk left a pile of turds some-where, people just waited for City Hall to clean it up, so naturally no one could have cared less about this sign, which would probably stay there until the wind

The Bridegroom Was a Dog

7

Missing Heels

63

The Gotthard Railway

129

ripped it to shreds and blew it away.

Anyway, the children all loved the Kitamura School, which they nicknamed the "Kitabooboo School"; in fact, so many wanted to go there it had become something of a fad, and even if it failed to improve some kids' grades, with all the stories these days about youngsters enrolled in cram schools they hated but actually spending the time in Game Centers, it was a relief to mothers, knowing they didn't have that to worry about with the Kitamura School, so most didn't let the strange rumors bother them, and when someone occasionally was heard saying she'd *never* send one of her children to a place like that, the others would tell her not to get so excited about some idle gossip which was only a kid's imagination to start with, blown out of all proportion, and since children can't really tell the difference between a little dirt and downright obscenity and tend to get things mixed up anyway, it was best not to believe everything they said, etc., etc.

Take, for example, what some grade school kids were reporting to their mothers about "snot paper": "Miss Kitamura says wiping your nose with snot paper you've already used once is nice, because it's so soft and warm and wet, but when you use it a third time to wipe yourself when you go to the bathroom, it feels even better." Mothers blushed to hear this from a son or daughter of theirs, wanting to scold but not sure exactly why or how, and in the end just telling them, "You mustn't say 'snot paper,' it's 'tissue,'" only to find that, no matter how determined they were not to imagine their child's beautiful teacher sitting on the toilet wiping herself with that lovely moist tissue, Miss Kitamura's smiling face invariably rose before them. And this, in turn, would remind them what the head teacher at the elementary school had said about her: "It's unusual for a beautiful woman to look that happy. I thought traditional beauties were supposed to be sad and lonely." Regardless of whether rumors about the head teacher's being distantly related to Mitsuko Kitamura were true or not, the mothers talked themselves into believing that if that straitlaced old schoolmarm said Mitsuko was beautiful, she couldn't be all that "dirty," and some even thought Mitsuko might be telling her pupils about "dirty" things on purpose, for educational reasons. And besides, none of the kids who had heard Mitsuko talk about the virtues of using "snot paper" three times followed suit and picked up an unhygienic habit; on the contrary, they were as wasteful as ever, rolling out reams of toilet paper so they could use just a few sheets at the end, and compared to the stories you heard about kids who competed with their little brothers to see who could pull the most tissues out of the box in the shortest time and then sent the whole wad fluttering down from the fifth floor window, Mitsuko Kitamura's lecture on "snot paper" began to sound like a serious lesson in frugality. So in the end no one took their children out of the Kitamura School because of the talk about "snot paper"; in fact, long after the kids had forgotten all about it, many mothers found that it came back to them every time they went to the toilet, and some wondered if there wasn't a softer, moister kind of paper they could use instead of this machine-made stuff, which felt awfully dry and scratchy sometimes.

What really stimulated their sensitivity in this area was the story the kids brought home about a princess and her dog. "Maybe the only story you know about a human being marrying an animal is 'The Crane Wife,' but there's another one called 'The Bridegroom Was a Dog,'" Miss Kitamura began, and the children listened carefully until the end, but the tale was so long that the younger ones got mixed up when they tried to tell it at home, and the older ones were too embarrassed to repeat it, so curious mothers were left to piece together the fragments they'd overheard for themselves, but, anyway, the story went like this. Once upon a time there was a little princess who was still too young to wipe herself after she went to the lavatory, and the woman assigned to look after her was too lazy to do it for her, so she used to call the princess's favorite black dog and say, "If you lick her bottom clean, one day she'll be your bride," and in time the princess herself began looking forward to that day....

Up to this point in the story, the children's accounts all matched each other, but there were various versions of what happened next: some said, for instance, that one day the black dog kidnapped the princess and took her deep into the forest, where he finally married her, while others said the princess's parents flew into a rage when they happened to catch the black dog licking their daughter's bottom, and sent both of them into exile on a desert island. The forest version had a hunter who killed the black dog when the princess wasn't looking and married her himself, after which the princess, though puzzled at first as to why the dog should suddenly have vanished and this hunter appeared in his place, lived happily with her new husband until one night he mumbled something in his sleep about having killed the animal, whereupon she promptly picked up his gun and shot him dead. The desert island version also had a further episode in the princess's life: she gave birth to a son, after which the black dog got sick and died, so to keep the family line from dying out the princess had relations with her son and bore more children. This arrangement she cleverly brought about by telling the boy one morning: "Go around the island to the other side and take the first woman you meet there as your wife," and while he was following the coastline in one direction, she herself set out in the other, and when the son met his mother on the far side of the island he slept with her without knowing who she was.

To the children listening, who didn't even know the word "incest," all this seemed perfectly natural, and it wasn't long before they'd forgotten all about it, whereas the part about the black dog obeying the lazy woman and licking the princess's bottom clean left a far more vivid impression, as you could tell by the way they lapped at their ice cream cones, barking between licks, or slobbered on the palms of their hands while they did their homework, which made their mothers sick, and started them thinking that it might be better to stop sending the kids to Miss Kitamura's after all before they got *really* strange, but then someone who was taking a class in folklore at the Culture Center swore she'd seen that story in one of her books, so it must be authentic, which was a comforting thought to the other mothers, one of whom said that any teacher who could get her pupils so interested in stories that weren't even in the textbooks was certainly unique, and although the word "unique" didn't sound quite right, most of them tended to agree, and there was a general sigh of relief.

Even so, since none of the mothers—either those who had grown up in the oldest part of Tokyo or the newer suburbs of Tama or Yamanote, or even those who hailed from the provinces to the north or west— ever remembered hearing a folk tale like that, some wondered whether Mitsuko Kimura hadn't spent time wandering around Southeast Asia, or maybe even as far away as Africa, which led to new speculations about her past.

"Maybe she was a hippie. They say she plays the fiddle, you know. That's probably what she was doing— riding around in the back of a caravan, playing the fiddle," said a mother in her mid-twenties, obviously mistaking "hippie" for "gypsy," but the word "hippie" suddenly reminded one of the older women of something:

"A while ago I was moving an old chest and found a

weekly magazine underneath it that I hadn't seen for years—a real relic it was—and there was an advertisement in it for a natural aphrodisiac made from dried eggplants that could be ordered from something called the Hippie Shop Kitamura. You don't suppose that was Miss Kitamura?" and so the rumors grew broader and deeper, and when another mother mentioned having seen a face that looked exactly like Mitsuko's on a wanted poster for a group of terrorists at the airport, some began to imagine that she'd been in hiding all these years, but then someone else assured them that she was just an ordinary teacher who'd been running the same kind of school in the Kansai area until she came here, which was enough to satisfy some of them.

One thing everybody knew for a fact was that Mitsuko Kitamura was thirty-nine, because every child knew how much fun it was to embarrass a woman teacher by asking her age, and that this was a bit of information that would never fail to interest their mothers, so when Miss Kitamura promptly told them "Thirty-nine" in answer to their questions, they duly reported it when they went home, which was why everyone at least knew that much about her, even though none of them had the faintest idea what she'd been doing until she suddenly moved into that house just a few years ago, when a family of farmers who had lived in the area for generations sold some land to build themselves a condominium near the station, and were about to tear down their old residence when Mitsuko Kitamura, wearing a white dress, appeared out of nowhere on a mountain bike and, claiming to be an old friend of one of their relations, asked if she could rent the house for ten years. Soon after this request was granted, she opened up her school, but to the folks around there it seemed pretty strange that such a stubborn old cuss as that farmer should give in so easily to a woman who came from god knows where, so for a while there was talk about her being a mistress he'd had stashed away; but when the locals actually saw her, she didn't look the type at all, dressed in shabby farming trousers with stylish sunglasses, and after seeing her sitting under the cherry tree happily reading a novel in Polish, no one could tell what kind of family she came from, and besides, when a woman doesn't have any children, the age of thirty-nine—past youth yet not quite over the hill—makes it hard to know what category to put her in, so eventually people thereabouts got tired of gossiping and decided to leave her alone, which just goes to show that the farming community wasn't nearly as keen on rumor-mongering as the housewives in the apartment complex.

The town where all this happened was made up of two distinct areas to the north and south: in the north were the modern housing developments that had sprung up along the railway with the station at its hub, while the southern district that lined the Tama River had prospered since ancient times, and yet many people in the Tama region didn't even know it existed, even though the public housing complexes that drew people to the north had only been in existence for about thirty years, whereas the south was *really* old, with the remains of ancient pit houses discovered near the river—human dwellings that dated back farther than you could imagine—and a traditional rice-growing culture that the farmers had kept alive until the introduction of cadmium rice in the 1960s, not to mention an old stone marker carved with the words "Eight *ri* from Nihonbashi" to show where a hamlet with a cluster of inns for travelers along the Old Tokaido Road had once flourished. Until the Kitamura School opened, the youngsters from the new apartment complex had seldom visited the southern area, with all its old houses that had survived the bombing in the war, except for the occasional sketching competition or science excursion to observe frogs, but nowadays, as though escaping the herds of people at home, they would hurry toward the Tama River on the appointed day, cross the highway, pass by the grounds of the local shrine, cut quietly across a plum grove, slip through the gap in the fence around Mitsuko's house and pop up in her garden, where the first to arrive would find Miss Kitamura, not sitting at her desk waiting for them, but calmly sewing on a button, reading a book, or cutting her toenails.

One day when three second-grade girls came proudly showing off a praying mantis they'd caught on the way, Mitsuko was kneeling on the tatami wearing a thread-bare pink tank top with what looked like brown rags on her bare shoulders, and when they asked: "What's that, Miss?" she calmly answered: "It's a plaster I made out of chicken shit." Ignoring the chorus of "Oh, yuck! Gross!" she went on, "Last night at Ueno Station I ran into a old friend, and while we were talking I realized what a bastard he'd turned into since I'd seen him last, and I got so fed up and depressed that my shoulders are stiff today, and chicken shit's the only thing that'll loosen them up."

The girls came closer, squealing in horror at the first whiff of the stuff, but they soon got used to it, their interest now shifting to the peach-colored tank top, about which they said quite openly: "You'd better buy a new one, Miss. That one's all raggedy," to which Mitsuko replied, as though everybody wore their clothes for as long as she did: "Oh? But it's only been seven years since I bought it."

The girls went crazy at first, clapping and jumping up and down as they chanted, "Raggedy! Raggedy!" but before long their attention turned to the breasts that were visible through the thin pink material. "The boys'll be here soon, Miss. What're you going to do then?" they said.

Laughing, Mitsuko slipped the strap of the tank top off her right shoulder and, taking her ample breast out to show them, answered: "Here's what I'll do."

Though they all shrieked "Oooh! Nasty!" it wasn't often they got a thrill like this, and when they begged her to do it again, she gave them two encores, but refused the third time, saying: "If you like to look at boobs that much, why don't you ask your mothers to show you theirs?" But then the girl who was thought to be the shyest of the three went right up to Mitsuko and pulled down both her straps, and just as the breasts came popping out like blowfish to a rousing cheer from the other two, the boys arrived.

Oddly enough, perhaps, far from sharing the girls' delight, the lads took one look and beat a hasty retreat through the hole in the fence; though they always seemed to get a kick out of watching girls cringe and squeal, *that* sort of female behavior was unsettling, and besides, they felt let down somehow to discover their teacher had such big breasts, so there they were, moping behind the fence, when Miss Kitamura, dressed in a proper blouse, came out to get them, took them by the hand, and led them back to the veranda, where there was no sign of either the pink tank top or the smelly plaster, and the little desks and chairs were neatly lined up as usual.

One day there was a new pupil at the Kitamura School, a third-grader named Fukiko. For some reason, the boys never passed her desk without smearing snot on her notebook, which was apparently what they always did at school, too. This neither angered Fukiko nor made her cry. The other girls never spoke to her or even glanced in her direction, so perhaps they failed to notice, or were pretending not to. That first day, Miss Kitamura just stared vaguely into space with big, watery eyes which, either because of nearsightedness or lack of sleep, didn't seem to focus on anything for the first hour of class until one of the boys smeared some snot on Fukiko's notebook for the third time, when she sud-

denly went over, grabbed his arm, and dragged him to
the cabinet, giving him such a shock that he must have
thought she was going to hit him, for he pulled his
neck in between his shoulders and closed his eyes, but
when he cautiously opened them again, Mitsuko had
taken out a blue notebook with a picture of a fox on
the cover, and, handing it to the boy, who stood there
stiff as a board, said:

"You should wipe your snot on your own notebook.
But then you wouldn't be able to read what you'd
written, so use this instead."

The other kids sat there in a daze, watching, but as
soon as the principle of the "snot book" began to sink
in they were all clamoring for one of their own, and
since there was only one left in Mitsuko's cabinet, it was
decided that the rest would get theirs the following
week, so the ruckus finally quieted down.

After class the following week, five girls were squatting in a circle in the garden staring at the ground, so
engrossed they'd apparently forgotten to go home, and
when Mitsuko, wondering what was up, went over to
join them, she discovered they were watching ten ants
drag a dead mayfly into their nest, having a terrible
time since the entrance was too small, which was when

she noticed Fukiko walking away without even stopping to see what the others were doing.

"Why don't you girls ever talk to Fukiko?" she asked.

Although none of them seemed to understand the question at first, one finally spoke up, as if she'd suddenly remembered the word she was trying to think of.

"Because she's strange."

"What's strange about her?" Mitsuko asked again.

And another piped up: "Well, she never washes her hair, and sometimes she doesn't even wear socks."

That was enough to get the rest going.

"She's fat."

"And she has a Snoopy pencil case but it's a fake."

"And she can't play dodgeball."

"And they say her father's weird."

"Oh, yeah, he hangs around in Game Centers and stuff like that."

After listening for a while, lost in thought, Mitsuko suddenly ran back into the house and retreated behind the sliding doors, slamming them behind her.

One August day soon after school had let out for the summer, a man of twenty-seven or -eight came calling at the Kitamura School with an old-fashioned leather suitcase but not a trace of sweat on him despite the hot sun beating down from above, and although he didn't look like a friend of Mitsuko's, with his closely cropped hair, immaculate white shirt, neatly creased trousers and polished leather shoes, he seemed to know all about her house, for he walked straight into the garden through the gap in the fence, and when he saw Mitsuko repairing her mountain bike, half-naked, her hair disheveled, he went right up to her and said:

"I'm here to stay."

Mitsuko's eyes widened and rolled upward, her mouth dropped open and she forgot to close it, and since she couldn't think what to say, she kept touching her throat with her fingertips, while the man silently put his suitcase down on the veranda, took off his wristwatch, and gave it two or three hard shakes as though to get the water out of it.

"Did you get my telegram?" he asked with a knowing laugh.

Unable to take in what was happening, Mitsuko stared blankly up at him and shook her head, furrowing her brow as though trying to think, so the man introduced himself in an even clearer tone:

"You can call me Taro. Under the circumstances, it mightn't be advisable to use my real name, but I can't think of any other."

Still in a daze, Mitsuko nodded weakly, and then, as though he'd suddenly thought of something, the man took her by the hand and, like a host inviting her into his own home, escorted her to the veranda, where he removed those fine leather shoes with a single shake of each ankle, without even bothering to stoop to untie them, before stepping up onto the wooden floor, and the strangest thing was that even so, when Mitsuko looked down, she saw the shoes neatly lined up on the stone below. He then took Mitsuko's waist in his large palms, which were neither hot nor cold nor the least bit sweaty, and lightly lifted her.

"Did you get my telegram?" he asked again.

This time Mitsuko hurriedly shook her head, where-upon the man slipped off her shorts as easily as drawing a handkerchief out of his sleeve, laid her on her back, and very politely, still in his shirt and pants, fitted his body on top of hers, then, gently pressing his canine teeth against the delicate skin of her neck, began suck-ing noisily, with Mitsuko's face growing paler all the while until she suddenly flushed crimson and the beads of sweat standing out on her forehead got sticky from the shock of feeling a thing with both the flexibility and indifference of a vegetable slide into her vagina, but as she writhed, struggling to get away, he flipped her over and, easily grabbing her thighs, one in each hand, raised them up and began licking her rectum, now poised precariously in midair. The sheer size of his tongue, the amount of saliva dripping from it, and the heavy panting were all literally extraordinary; and besides, even in this sweltering heat, the huge hands that gripped Mitsuko's thighs neither trembled nor grew the least bit moist no matter how long they held her that way, and when at last he gently pulled her up into a sitting position, the dark eyes that gazed into hers were tranquil, without so much as a droplet of sweat on the forehead or nose, and since his hair was as neat as ever, she reached out without thinking and touched it, only to find it as coarse as the bristles of a scrubbing brush, the skin beneath as smooth and strong as cowhide, and while she sat there as though in a trance, stroking his head, the man quietly, seriously, returned her gaze, until on a sudden impulse, leaving Mitsuko still naked from the waist down, he ran into the kitchen and started stir-frying some bean sprouts.

When she finally came to herself, Mitsuko put her shorts back on and went into the kitchen to find a meal ready, the table neatly set with plates and bowls for rice and soup, all looking like doll's dishes in the man's big hands. He'd been sitting there waiting for her, and at the sight of her let out a cheer, then tucked into the rice in a manner that was somehow refined but frighteningly energetic, wolfing it down so fast that his bowl was empty before Mitsuko had even picked up her chopsticks, then quickly helping himself to a second bowlful, which he devoured in no time, and when she gave him a reproachful look, he licked the bowl clean with his long tongue, then suddenly stood up and, taking a rag from the suitcase he'd left on the veranda, rinsed it, wrang it out at the kitchen sink, and began scrubbing the wooden corridor. As Mitsuko's eyes moved back and forth between her rice bowl, still more than half full, and the man washing the floor, with the muscles in his bottom pumping up and down in perfect rhythm as he pushed the rag along on all fours, he looked so funny she burst out laughing, and as she giggled and ate, the floorboards began to give off a dull sheen, and by the time she finished he'd taken a duster from the suitcase and begun dusting the rooms inside, easily reaching corners so high up that Mitsuko would have had to stand on a chair to get to them, scooping up cobwebs in his hands as they fluttered down and gobbling them like cotton candy, and though for a while she sat there motionless among the motes of dust, sparkling in the western sunlight, when she saw him

take out a blue fold-up broom and start sweeping the
tatami, she went out into the garden where she wouldn't
be in his way, and was gazing at the bike she'd been
repairing earlier, standing there with a tube dangling
wantonly from the tire like an intestine, when she heard
someone greet her:

"Good afternoon, Miss."

She looked up in surprise to see two of her pupils
standing on the other side of the fence in red swimming
trunks.

"Who's that man, Miss?" they asked bluntly.

Not knowing how to answer, Mitsuko tried to gloss
over it with a simple, "Oh, just somebody I know,"
which didn't satisfy the children.

"Why's he cleaning your house?" they wanted to
know, but as Mitsuko was fumbling for another reply,
luckily they heard the distant voice of another child
calling, and raced off in that direction.

Not that the two boys forgot what they'd seen—far
from it; in fact, when one of them got home he ran up
the apartment steps two at a time, and without stopping
to catch his breath or call out "I'm home!" went straight
to his mother with the news.

"When we went by Miss Kitamura's on the way
home from the pool, a man was cleaning her house."

"A man? What kind of man?"

He didn't know, really, but finally managed to say: "Like Superman, sort of. Real big and kind of scary."

"About how old was he?"

"Around twenty, or maybe thirty, I guess."

His mother laughed, thinking some nephew of Miss Kitamura's must have come up to Tokyo and found the house so dirty he decided to do something about it; people might say young men were turning into sissies these days, but you had to admire a man who liked a clean house.

"What do you think—would a young unmarried man nowadays go so far as to clean a single woman's house for her?" she asked when she ran into another mother from the next building and told her all about it, but the other woman cocked her head and said:

"A nephew? I wonder. Seems more likely City Hall has sent in a social worker. A place with that many children running in and out has to be sanitary, you know."

As the two women talked, a certain suspicion did, admittedly, arise in their minds, but it was left unsaid, until several days later the same child reported seeing the man again when he'd passed Miss Kitamura's place on the way home from the pool that evening; this time he was in the garden "cutting the grass," which didn't

sound right at all, and even though the Kitamura School
was out for the summer, Mitsuko's name was soon on
mothers' lips throughout the apartment complex, along
with the phrase "cutting the grass," which took on a
special meaning, though no one could have told you
exactly what it was, and although Mitsuko herself didn't
know the content of the rumors, she was sure there
were plenty floating around, since the man she was now
used to calling "Taro" had been seen by the same pupil
twice in a row, and it wasn't just a matter of "having
been seen," either, for while the first time he'd just been
cleaning the house, which was all right, on the second
occasion he'd been sitting in the grass about to tickle
her rectum with a bunch of clover when the boy's face
had appeared through the fence, startling Mitsuko, who
was lying face down but now sat up, burying her legs in
the grass and yanking her skirt down, while Taro, apparently not noticing the child, tried to lift up the hem
she'd just pulled down, and then, still oblivious to the
boy staring at them with ever widening eyes, picked her
up and planted her firmly between the branches of the
cherry tree.

If his physical strength was somewhat out of the
ordinary, so was the rhythm of his days, for while the
sun was out he'd lie around sleeping, but at six in the

evening he'd be up cleaning the house and making a sumptuous meal, and by the time he and Mitsuko were finished eating, he would suddenly be full of energy, ready for lovemaking, after which he always went out alone into the darkness to spend half the night running around god knows where, only returning—without a sound—just as Mitsuko was about to go to sleep, but since Taro then kept her up until dawn with his love-making again, Mitsuko could no longer get up in the morning and would be dozing off all day, except when some salesman marched into the garden unannounced and she'd have to get up in a hurry, but unlike Taro, who was always alert the minute he awoke, with his eyes wide open and his hair as neat as if he'd just combed it, Mitsuko would emerge bleary-eyed, her hair sticking out in all directions, so that the person outside the door would blurt out: "Sorry. Seems I've caught you at a bad time," at which Mitsuko would blush, not knowing how to explain, and while she was busy making lame excuses, the woman who ran the general store in the neighborhood was telling everyone she met that Mitsuko Kitamura had "got herself a man," an odd phrase that the housewives from the apartment complex re-frained from using because they found it rather crude, but when they tried something lighter like "Miss Kitamura has a boyfriend," it sounded like a joke, so for lack of anything better they ended up saying, "It seems there's a young man living at Miss Kitamura's," which you could take to mean anything you chose, and though they were all dying to see this young man for themselves, during the summer vacation the house-wives had no reason to venture into the southern part of town, so they sent their children to the pool, remind-ing them to be sure to stop by Miss Kitamura's to say hello on the way back, sometimes even sending along some sweets for her, but these kids, though they looked the picture of innocence, were actually just as keen to see Taro themselves, for the very sight of him gave them that thrill children get from seeing something they're not supposed to, and even if they didn't catch Mi-tsuko doing anything in particular, even if Taro was just sitting on a stone in a corner of the garden staring blankly into space, their hearts beat faster, and some didn't so much drop in to see Miss Kitamura on the way home from the pool as go swimming just so they could catch a glimpse of Taro.

Taro didn't mind the children staring at him in the least. Although he got nervous when dogs or cats wan-dered into the garden, people he simply ignored, which worried Mitsuko, who found herself wondering one day what would happen after August when classes started again, for the Kitamura School was her only source of income. Though half asleep, she was still pursuing this thought when she looked at the clock and saw it was already past five, so she sat up and glanced around the room to discover that Taro, who had appeared out of nowhere, was right in front of her, burying his head between her knees, to smell her, she assumed, as she could tell by the sound that he was breathing through his nose, and he went on doing this until her legs started to go numb and she shifted to one side and tried to stand up, which was difficult, of course, with Taro clinging to her like that, holding on so long in fact that Mitsuko thought she'd go out of her mind, but she knew that he never got tired of sniffing an odor he liked. Although he didn't have a job—didn't do anything, really, except take care of the laundry, cooking, and cleaning—he was never bored enough to resort to reading or watching television, and his principal hobby was smelling her body; when he got started he could sometimes keep at it for an hour or more, which at first bored Mitsuko to tears, but in time made her realize that her body was always slightly damp with perspiration and that, far from being odorless, her sweat carried various faint but distinct aromas not unlike those of seaweed, shellfish, citrus fruit, milk, and iron, depending on minor shifts in mood, so that when she was surprised by something, for instance, she'd notice a certain odor in the air around her and think, "Ah. I must be surprised," which is how she got into the habit of smelling herself as she reacted to things.

Oddly enough, Taro wasn't at all attracted to breasts, and never touched Mitsuko's; although kissing didn't interest him either, sucking certainly did, but the spot he always chose for that was Mitsuko's neck, which he'd attack like a vampire, leaving a number of reddish-purple, doughnut-shaped marks, which Mitsuko would have to hide, in spite of the heat, by wrapping an Indian cotton scarf around her neck, making her sweat all the more; and when she caught sight of herself in a mirror and saw how red and swollen her face was, with dry lips and a rounder nose than before, she realized she'd never seen herself looking this bad—all because of Taro, which seemed strange, but perhaps having someone so strongly attached to you did actually ruin your looks, and besides, he never looked her up and down in the coolly appraising way that other people did anyway, while Mitsuko, who at one time hadn't minded being appraised like that, now had him always grabbing her and holding on for dear life, which left her no time to repair the damage.

One day a group of seven or eight third-graders dropped by with their mothers on the way back from an outing, to bring her a watermelon, so Mitsuko busied herself pouring iced barley tea and setting out cushions, glancing nervously around the room all the while, even though everything, thanks to Taro, looked neat enough and the tea glasses sparkled like crystal, so to anyone ignorant of the circumstances there would have seemed no need to worry, but Mitsuko didn't know what she'd do if Taro, who was asleep in the next room, were suddenly to get up; on top of which, these proper-looking housewives seemed to have brought an invasion of odors with them, waves of sweat, perfume, the paste they use for pickling vegetables, detergent, blood, tooth powder, insecticide, coffee, fish, cough medicine, band-aids, and nylons, which confused her completely, making it impossible to distinguish the subtle aroma that hovered around her own body, without which she couldn't be sure how she was feeling, so although it was only natural that she should be annoyed with these people for bursting in on her with no warning, without the smell to prove it her own feelings didn't seem real to her, which upset her all the more. As Mitsuko joined halfheartedly in the conversation, taking care not to breathe through her nose, wishing they would all leave soon, the clock on the wall struck six, and at that very moment the sliding doors opened and Taro appeared.

He was wearing nothing but a cotton summer kimono, which opened at the front when he put his right leg forward, but while the mothers, of course, pretended they hadn't seen a thing, one of the kids cried out "Wow! Awesome!"—though it wasn't altogether clear what he was referring to.

There was no reaction from Taro, so perhaps he hadn't heard, but one of the mothers whispered "Oh my god, it's Iinuma," then promptly clammed up, which sounded ominous to Mitsuko, yet no one else apparently had noticed, for they all started saying things like, "We've been making such a nuisance of ourselves. We'd better be running along now," as if they knew it was about time for Taro to begin his nightly routine, and although Mitsuko had intended to be polite and ask them to stay a little longer, she accidentally bit her tongue and missed her chance, so with Taro just standing there without so much as saying hello, an awkward silence ensued, until the women, shooting disapproving looks at this rude young man who still refused to speak, stood up and started dithering about, preparing to leave, while a Mrs. Orita, the person who had whispered "Oh my god, it's Iinuma," watched a fly buzzing around her as though it were a bee, following it with frightened eyes straight out the door ahead of all the rest, apparently only too happy to get away.

After seeing them off, Mitsuko stood vacantly in the doorway for a while, but at the sound of Taro washing the glasses in the kitchen, she stirred herself and got a fan, which she began waving wildly about, trying to chase out all the intrusive smells, occasionally stopping to think, then fanning again, repeating the pattern over and over again.

After having sex with Mitsuko as usual, Taro went out, and a while later the phone rang. It was Mrs. Orita.

"I didn't get a chance to talk at your house with so many people around, but it's about that young man who's living with you; I just saw him for the first time today, but he looks so much like a fellow called Iinuma who used to work under my husband that I couldn't help wondering.... He was one of my husband's favorites, you see, but he disappeared three years ago, and his wife's been looking for him ever since, poor thing, so if that really *is* Iinuma, I'd like her to know."

At first Mitsuko answered coldly, "Yes ... yes," but as she listened the air seemed to close in on her and she found it hard to speak, so when the woman said, "I'm going to talk to Iinuma's wife and have her go see for herself," as though it were already decided, she couldn't object.

When Mrs. Orita asked, "Where did you meet that young man, anyway?" she fudged it, since telling what had really happened was out of the question.

"Oh, just by chance; someone introduced him, and asked me to rent him a room. But tell me, how do you write 'Iinuma'?"

Ignoring her question, Mrs. Orita proceeded to explain at great length what sort of person he was, so Mitsuko protested:

"But I'm not very interested in his character—sorry, it may seem odd, but I don't really want to hear about it." And she started to put the phone down, then reluctantly picked it up again and, to help her endure the steady stream of chatter pouring into her ear, held her head in her left hand and closed her eyes, patiently waiting for it to end.

According to Mrs. Orita, Taro Iinuma had gone to work for the pharmaceutical company her husband was with after graduating from a university in Tokyo, and though her husband had taken a liking to him from the start, if you'd asked him why, he wouldn't have been able to tell you, but if forced to give a reason he would have said it was because young Iinuma was the kind of guy who could accept your point of view—could say, "I see what you mean," without sounding snide or insincere in any way. For example, one day not long after he'd joined the company, Orita had seen him in the parking lot leaning against a car with one shoe off, wiping the sole with a handkerchief embroidered with violets, and when he'd asked him what he was doing, Iinuma had said: "I stepped on a worm and got my shoe all dirty." Looking at the expanse of gray asphalt, Orita had shouted, "How could there be worms in a place like this!" to which Iinuma had replied: "I see what you mean," and stopped wiping right then and there. Afterward, though, when he was telling his wife about it, Orita had said he now realized that Iinuma had probably stepped in a pile of dog shit but for some reason couldn't come out and say it, and that was why the poor fellow had lied.

Poor Iinuma—he was often the butt of his co-workers' jokes, too. For example, the year he joined, he never used company pencils but always brought his own with him, like an elementary school kid, and no matter how many times he was asked about it, he refused to say why, so they all started teasing him, saying things like: "He'll only use pencils with Miss Kitty on them." Orita had taken him drinking and, when he'd loosened up a bit, asked him about it, too, first assuring him that he didn't have to talk about it unless he really wanted to, so, on condition that Orita promise not to tell anyone else, Iinuma had explained his behavior to him: the "reason," it seemed, was that the girl who sat across from him had the habit of chewing on her pencils when no one was looking, and since she was always leaving them around, she often came to borrow one from Iinuma, but that wasn't all—she'd sometimes leave pencils on Iinuma's desk in return for the ones he'd lent her, and since company pencils were all the same, there was always the possibility he might use one that she had chewed on, and the very thought of it made his palms itch.

"I envy you, getting pencils a pretty girl's chewed on," Orita had said, trying to make a joke of it. "Do they still have her spit and tooth marks on them?" But far from relaxing, Iinuma had stiffened noticeably, which made Orita realize that since kidding wouldn't work, he'd have to give it to him straight. "You'll never get anywhere if you let little things like that bother you. You've got to stop being so nervous," he told him, and Iinuma had replied, in that special way of his, "I see what you mean," and stopped bringing his own pencils to work the very next day, much to Orita's relief, but while he'd felt pleased with himself for having given such good advice and even more well-disposed toward Iinuma for taking it, there had been various other incidents after that, such as the time he noticed that whenever Iinuma sat down he shifted his bottom this way and that on the seat of the chair, and no matter how hard his colleagues tried not to laugh, they couldn't help exchanging winks and snickers, until Orita decided to do something about it, and told Iinuma about a doctor he'd once seen for his hemorrhoids, but Iinuma had said that wasn't the problem: no, he didn't have hemorrhoids, it was just that his skin was so delicate that when he used the toilet seats in the company men's room, he broke out in a rash, and since Orita didn't know what to do, he spoke to his wife, who told him there was something you could buy to put over a toilet seat—a plastic bag, shaped like a long sock—and when he suggested that Iinuma try it, he'd looked surprised and said, "I see what you mean," then went out and bought one of them, and started using it.

Four years earlier, Iinuma had been engaged to Ryoko, a thin, soft-spoken woman who looked a bit like a fox; she worked in the same section, and since she was four years younger and only a high school graduate, Orita had felt confident she wouldn't frighten even a timid man like Iinuma, but still wasn't sure how the young man felt about his coming marriage, for he had the impression that although Ryoko was happy enough, Iinuma wasn't so enthusiastic, and he wondered if Ryoko had found out about some weakness of Iinuma's, making him feel obliged to marry her even though there was someone else he liked better, which was a bit worrying, so he'd asked him about it in a roundabout way, and since it had seemed that wasn't the case, he'd let it go, but though the wedding had gone off without a hitch and nothing noteworthy had happened afterward, about a year later, without a word of warning either to Ryoko or the company, Iinuma had suddenly disappeared.

It wasn't as though he hadn't had a chance to talk to Iinuma alone after the marriage, but they'd been busy at work that year, and the two or three times they'd gone drinking Iinuma hadn't had much to say; in fact, he had only mentioned Ryoko once, when Orita remembered asking: "How's Ryoko? Bet she's a good wife." Looking as though he really didn't want to say it, Iinuma had replied: "Sometimes when I get home, I find my tooth-brush has been broken into little bits. It's surprising how strong even small women are, isn't it?" Not knowing how to answer but thinking he should at least try to be encouraging, Orita had said, "Sounds like a woman you can depend on," but Iinuma had just hung his head, and when he spoke again it was to ask: "Mr. Orita, do you like *miso* soup with fried bean curd? They say foxes do, but I don't," which made the older man say sternly, "Look, if she's always fixing something you don't like, why don't you tell her about it? There's no reason to put up with it," but Iinuma had mumbled, "No, well, actually she doesn't make that soup, it's just that..." The words then trailed off, leaving Orita patiently waiting for him to continue: "... it *smells* like she does. I don't like smells of any kind, and I can't stand sleeping closed up in a little room with another ani-mal, even a hamster. You can hear them breathing, you know. And the rhythm is completely different from mine, so just listening to it makes me feel like I'm suffocat-ing."

This, to Mitsuko's relief, was enough to convince her that the man Mrs. Orita was talking about was definitely not her Taro, who loved smells so much he couldn't live without them.

"All right, then, please tell Ryoko she's welcome to come over any time and see if this guy's her husband," she said into the phone, and despite an obvious disappointment at hearing Mitsuko sound so cool and reasonable about it, Mrs. Orita called Ryoko immediately, explained how to get to the house, and strongly recommended that she go, only to find that Ryoko, too, was perfectly calm, asking, "Does Miss Kitamura like fruit? What do you think I should take her?" which wasn't at all the sort of thing Mrs. Orita had expected her to be worried about, so she hung up feeling rather put out.

It was an evening late in August when Ryoko went to see Mitsuko Kitamura: the sky was heavy and so swollen with moisture it looked about to burst, and as the thunder rumbled like a lion growling deep in its throat and it suddenly grew dark, a small, thin figure with glittering eyes slipped into the garden through the break in the fence. Mitsuko thought it was a child at first, but closer up she saw a woman in her mid twenties, who, after a brief glance at Taro, sitting in a corner of the garden gazing blankly at the sky, stared Mitsuko in the face as she bowed and said:

"I'm Ryoko."

Just as Mitsuko hurried her into the house, large drops began to fall, bringing Taro slowly to his feet to join them inside, and since Ryoko's expression didn't change at all when she was looking him over, Mitsuko felt reassured, concluding as she poured her guest a glass of barley tea that Iinuma the missing husband and this Taro must be two different people after all, while Ryoko now kept her eyes fixed on Mitsuko, not even glancing in Taro's direction when he stood up, went into the back room, and closed the sliding doors behind him. By now the evening shower was a downpour, but when Mitsuko got up to close the shutters Ryoko suddenly pounced on her, grabbing both ankles with a strength you wouldn't have expected of her, so that Mitsuko flipped onto her back on the *tatami*, and found herself staring into Ryoko's eyes, which looked so much like Taro's it shocked her. Pinning her down, Ryoko pulled the scarf from around Mitsuko's neck, sniffed at the reddish-purple, doughnut-shaped marks that were hidden beneath it, and asked in a harsh voice:

"Did you get my telegram?"

Mitsuko shook her head like a child falsely accused of something until Ryoko took her hands away, and while Mitsuko was picking herself up off the floor, she took a blue name card from her handbag and said:

"Come to my house tomorrow."

It was so obviously an order that Mitsuko, unable to say no, just sat there in a daze, watching the rain drench the veranda, and by the time the evening sun had begun to reappear between the clouds, lighting up the strands of raindrops, Ryoko was nowhere to be seen.

Now alert but still unable to move, feeling as though she were tied up, Mitsuko eventually got up and went to the back room to see what Taro was doing, only to find that he, too, was no longer there.

The next day Mitsuko went to a neighboring town to visit Ryoko, who lived in an apartment complex which, except for a reddish tinge to the outside walls, was exactly like the one where Mitsuko's pupils lived, and following the numbers in the address—1-7-6-4— she found Ryoko's apartment, climbed the stairs to arrive in front of a door identical to the ones on either side, and rang the bell, but when Ryoko appeared looking meek and mild, the glitter of last night gone from her eyes, Mitsuko had no qualms about going in, nor did anything catch her eye as she surveyed the room, which smelled of fried bean curd, except perhaps for something on top of the dresser that looked like a bit of sacred rope, the kind that's hung in Shinto shrines to ward off evil, and as her eyes wandered over it she noticed Ryoko smirking in the background.

Ryoko proceeded to inform her that the man she'd gone to check out the day before was definitely her husband, but she had not been shocked by his disappearance three years earlier, nor was she still searching for him without a clue to his current whereabouts as the Oritas believed, for she saw him occasionally in passing, and knew that recently he'd been "playing around" at night with a man called Toshio Matsubara, whom she'd also met—and who had struck her as surprisingly ordinary, though certainly not dull—but she knew her husband must also have a woman he played around with during the day, and had been wanting to meet her, too, when Mrs. Orita had obliged by creating this opportunity. All this, however, was news to Mitsuko, to whom it came as a huge shock. Toshio Matsubara was her pupil Fukiko's father, and since he'd been raising her alone since the death of her mother some years before, it was he who had brought the girl to the Kitamura School to see about enrolling her, and though he was small and stout, with a loose, flabby face that made him look as if he might burst into tears at any moment, and despite having a right canine tooth missing which made him whistle his "s's" in an irritating way, he'd been very polite, seeming to trust Mitsuko's judgment completely, so she had soon warmed to him, and as they chatted away like old friends, she realized that he knew about all sorts of fascinating things like the life cycle of the crocodile and the structure of Indonesian houses, and someone told her later that he was good at his job as well, so he certainly didn't seem the type to be "playing around"; but since she didn't know exactly what Ryoko had meant by the term, she asked her.

"By 'playing around,' do you mean with women?"

"No, just the two of them," Ryoko said sharply.

"What exactly do they do?"

This question sent Ryoko into spasms of laughter, making all further inquiry impossible, so Mitsuko waited quietly until Ryoko started again on her disturbing monologue:

"That man is no longer the Taro Iinuma I married. My husband was a nervous, wishy-washy sort of person, who couldn't stand the touch of somebody else's skin, and who I'm sure I would have divorced long ago anyway, but though he apparently still likes to keep things tidy, the Taro I saw yesterday is a completely different person. There was an incident just before he disappeared that may have accounted for the change in him. Anyway, even though Taro's stopped being the man I was married to, there are one or two things about him that are still the same, so I thought if I decided to go back to him, I'd have to make myself physically as strong as he is now, which is why I started going to a *dojo*, but then as I got into training I found I was far more interested in that than in getting my husband back."

Still slightly bewildered, Mitsuko asked: "When you say 'training,' you mean something like Aikido?"

In the twinkling of an eye, Ryoko picked her up and laid her flat across the table, and while Mitsuko was flailing her legs and arms about, struggling to get down, she banged her knee against the wall, but hardly had time to yell "Ouch!" before Ryoko had her mouth on the spot, sucking at it like an octopus with loud smacking sounds until she'd drawn the pain right out.

"I feel I'm gradually turning into Taro somehow," Ryoko said, which made Mitsuko blush, and as she rubbed her knee, Ryoko told her about the incident three years earlier that may have been the catalyst for Taro's transformation.

On top of a nearby hill that wasn't yet covered with rows of new houses, a restaurant had just opened, and one Sunday afternoon Taro and Ryoko had tea and cheese cake there, and after buying a steak and some sauce to take home, they started down the hill behind the restaurant, thinking it might be nice to walk to the station, and as they strolled along the lonely path through the woods they thought they heard an odd noise behind them, like the rumble of an engine, but when they turned around there was nothing there, just some old pipes stacked up in a clearing where some trees had been chopped down, so they went on, turning onto a narrow road, where they heard the same rumbling sound, this time coming from the waist-high grass growing in the fields on either side of them, and just as Ryoko muttered "I wonder what that is?" some dogs leapt out at them, one after another, but seeing they weren't very big, only about the size of Shibas, Ryoko wasn't frightened at first—even though thoughts like "They're not wearing collars, so they must be strays," and "They're growling" did cross her mind— until one of the dogs jumped on Taro, and the moment he screamed, the others followed suit (except for one that went after the bag with the steak which he threw away as far as he could), sinking their teeth into his legs, refusing to let go, tearing his trousers to shreds as he yelled, "Stop it! Let me go! You're getting me all dirty!"

Ryoko ran back to the phone booth they'd passed to call the police, and waited there until some men from City Hall came with sticks and nets, but when she led them to the spot, the dogs had vanished, leaving Taro lying unconscious by the side of the road. After rushing him to a nearby hospital in a police car, they found that he had fifteen or sixteen bite marks on his legs, none of them fortunately very deep, and since he didn't appear to have rabies and soon regained consciousness, Ryoko felt they'd been pretty lucky—a feeling that lasted only until Taro's grandmother drove up in a taxi with a wild look in her eye and some dire warnings. "The boy's lost. An evil spirit's got him now," she announced before bursting into tears, while Taro's mother, who had arrived a little later, looked embarrassed and made excuses.

"You mustn't listen to Granny. She's always been superstitious, but lately she's joined one of those crazy new religions, and you never know what kind of nonsense she's going to come out with."

For some reason, hearing this made the back of Ryoko's earlobes turn cold as ice, and, grabbing Taro, she pulled him up and shook him. "You're not going to turn weird on me now, are you?" she yelled at him.

Perhaps shocked at the way she was behaving, Taro

said nothing, which only made things worse, until all
the irritation she'd been keeping in check exploded.
"Why don't you say something? Have you gone dumb?"
she yelled again.

From then on, Taro stopped talking altogether, which
drove Ryoko to new heights of anger, but when she
tried to break his silence by throwing dishes at him,
he finally left home. He didn't go far, however, as she
still saw him in the park or at the station, each time
looking more muscular, with a brighter gleam in his
eyes, moving with such agility that, more often than
not, he'd be gone before she had a chance to call out to
him.

Taro must have stopped going to work after that,
and when Mr. Orita called to ask what had happened,
she told him through her tears: "The fact is he's disappeared, and I don't know where he's gone." But it
wasn't sadness that made her cry, it was because she was
afraid he might wonder why she hadn't told anyone
until now and start asking some nasty questions, so
she'd chosen to play the role of a woman so heart-
broken she didn't know what she was doing, though her
real feelings toward Taro no longer involved anger but
jealousy, for compared to Taro, who looked fitter every
time she saw him, her own body moved so slowly and

awkwardly it seemed downright unattractive even to her, which was why she'd started "training."

In the end, Mitsuko left Ryoko's apartment without really understanding either what Taro and Toshio did when they "played around," or the nature of Ryoko's "training," but when she got home she looked at Taro and thought, so this guy used to be an ordinary wage slave, and felt the old excitement slipping away. After school started on September 1, however, the children came back, and Mitsuko was busy teaching from late afternoon on into the evening, while Taro started leaving during the day and not returning until after dark, which suited Mitsuko fine, since seeing him in broad daylight somehow disgusted her now; in the darkened house, in the middle of the night, she didn't mind, but for the rest of the time she wanted to rub him out of her life.

She developed a special fondness for Fukiko: before the vacation she'd merely wanted to protect her from all the bullying she got, but now she combed her hair and trimmed her nails, and told her to come an hour early so they could go over her schoolwork, and when Fukiko still did poorly, Mitsuko got as angry as if it had been herself. Fukiko, on the other hand, seemed to find

Mitsuko a little creepy, and refused to come early at first, making up stories about things she had to do, and hurrying home after class before Mitsuko had a chance to speak to her, as though she didn't want all this attention; so when Mitsuko cornered her one day and asked, "What do you do about dinner?" she just said, "My father gives me money," which didn't satisfy Mitsuko, who asked again, "And what do you spend it on?" Mitsuko's exasperated sigh when she heard the answer—"*Yakitori*, or cheeseburgers"—made the girl feel so embarrassed she burst into tears, so Mitsuko told her, "Starting tomorrow you'll eat with me," which didn't particularly please her but left her little choice, making her decide to start crying again, except now she couldn't stop; and as Mitsuko wiped away her tears, her resistance seemed to crumble and she buried her face in Mitsuko's bosom and cried her heart out, and since even her father, who didn't like people and warned her to stay away from them, never had a bad word to say about this woman, it didn't seem like such a bad thing to do.

So Fukiko forgot herself from time to time and began to depend on her. Every day after school, she would go over to Mitsuko's place, eat the dinner Taro made, and after he'd gone out, except for Thursdays when she had a class there with the other third-graders, either go outdoors to play or shut herself in the back room, until about five minutes before Taro was due home when, almost instinctively, she would leave. She was soon accustomed to this routine, and if she never smiled when she saw Mitsuko, she no longer ran away from her, while Mitsuko tried to draw her out by buying her books, but Fukiko hated books, and didn't really care for food, either, unless it was flavored with ketchup or mayonnaise, dawdling over the meals Taro cooked but feeling duty-bound to eat them, casting sly, sidelong glances at the cook himself, who seemed to fascinate her.

Fukiko wasn't a talkative child, but when asked a question, perhaps because she didn't really understand what the other person wanted to know, she'd sometimes go on about unrelated topics, such as the time Mitsuko said: "Your father knows about a lot of things, doesn't he? Once when he came here, he told me all about crocodiles. I bet he's been to lots of different countries."

Fukiko thought for a moment before replying, looking rather pleased with herself: "Dad's always saying he wants to go somewhere, but he just packs a suitcase and puts it by the bathroom door, and never goes anywhere. He says the last time he went on a trip was before he got the job he has now."

Mitsuko tried again: "He must be busy working," but Fukiko just cocked her head, without so much as a nod, and it occurred to Mitsuko that she'd never heard Fukiko use the word "busy," which was unusual for a child nowadays—she'd found that odd from the start.

Another time, when Mitsuko asked, "What does your father say about Taro?" Fukiko just gave her a dubious look and said, "Has he met Taro?" and since she could tell by the look in the eyes gazing up at her that the girl wasn't playing dumb, Mitsuko regretted having asked her in the first place.

You couldn't say Fukiko looked clever, gripping her chopsticks with her sticky fingers, pulling at her ears, or just sitting there, lost in thought as she slowly put her food in her mouth, and yet, watching her, Mitsuko often felt a love akin to irritation well up in her, so strong it hurt, and sometimes she even wished Taro would hurry up and leave so the two of them could be alone, not that they did anything special together; in fact, more often than not they'd end up quarreling, because Mitsuko would be determined to read to her, and Fukiko wanted no part of it, but when, for example, Mitsuko took Fukiko's blouse off so she could sew on the buttons that were hanging by a thread, the girl would sit there beside her, naked to the waist, intently watching the movements of her fingers, and after a while her head would be leaning against Mitsuko's shoulder, and when Mitsuko was sure she must have fallen asleep, she'd look over to find the child still gravely following the needle with her eyes, so Mitsuko would say:

"You like sewing on buttons better than reading, don't you?"

"That's because I'm not 'smart' like you."

This cheeky sort of remark only made Mitsuko angry again.

After she took the girl under her wing, the other kids stopped bullying her openly, but there were more nasty rumors going the rounds than ever before, especially one about Fukiko's father "swinging his hips" at the Game Center; this was an expression the junior high school boys used to refer to various things, but it had filtered down to the elementary school children, who were all using it now without knowing what it meant, and though it upset their mothers to overhear this sort of language, they didn't understand it either, and had no one to ask. When Mitsuko first heard it from Mrs. Orita, for some reason it cracked her up, not that *she* knew what it meant herself, it just sounded so funny, but Mrs. Orita frowned as though she thought she was laughing at her.

"Don't you think it needs looking into, though? After all, there's AIDS to worry about, too, you know."

Unable to see what she was getting at, Mitsuko blurted out: "Look into? What's there to look into?"

Mrs. Orita was quite fed up by now with Mitsuko, who had never once said anything that made sense to her, and in total exasperation started to say: "But don't you see? Your Taro—if …," then realized that since Taro didn't belong to Miss Kitamura, "your" was hardly appropriate, and that she was under no obligation to investigate the company he kept, either.

Beginning at last to catch on, Mitsuko said: "Oh, if that's what it is, there's nothing to worry about," meaning that since she wasn't sleeping with Taro any more, it made no difference to her what he did or with whom. But Mrs. Orita, who didn't have that sort of thing in mind at all, inquired disapprovingly:

"Hadn't you better sit down, the two of you, and have a good talk about this? Of course the best thing would be for Iinuma to go back to Ryoko, but if neither of them wants to start over again, Iinuma could divorce Ryoko, and then he'd be free to marry *you*, which seems a logical thing to do. Either way, doesn't it bother you to have him hanging around in gay bars?..."

Mitsuko started at the words "marry" and "gay bar," as it dawned on her that maybe the Game Centers the kids were always talking about were actually places gays went to, and she was the only one who didn't know. Even if that *were* the case, though, Taro's behavior no longer had much to do with her, so she replied:

"But what's wrong with that? There's nothing I can do about it anyway. And why on earth should he have to marry me?"

Mrs. Orita blinked. "Just what do you think he is— you and Ryoko both? Poor Iinuma! It isn't fair!" There were tears in her eyes when she left for home.

One weekend toward the end of September, the Oritas took their son to Mrs. Orita's parents' for a visit, and when they got off the train at Ueno Station on Sunday night, the boy squatted down on the platform, saying his gym shoe laces had got tangled up, which, as his mother soon saw, was indeed the case, with his left and right shoes actually tied together in a terrific knot, and while she was standing there waiting for him to sort out the mess and retie the laces properly, wondering how in the world things like this happened, she glanced over at the opposite platform, where she saw Taro Iinuma and Toshio Matsubara, each holding a suitcase, standing so close together their bodies touched, so she grabbed her husband by the arm, and though he stood there gawking around for a bit, he finally saw them too.

"Iinuma!" he called out.

Taro quickly spotted Mr. Orita and bowed politely, not the least bit flustered, and when Orita yelled, "Where're you going?" he answered in a clear, carrying voice: "Thank you for all your help."

Orita's "You idiot!" was drowned out by the express train coming in, hiding the two behind it. Leaving the luggage with his wife, Orita ran down the stairs and across to the other platform, but soon returned, out of breath, gasping:

"They got away. Let's call the police."

It was just as well his wife stopped him, for as even he soon realized, there was nothing criminal about their going on a trip together somewhere. What his wife said made much better sense.

"We've got to let Miss Kitamura know."

But when they called Mitsuko from the platform, no one answered the phone, so there was nothing to do but go home, where they tried again, but still with no result, which seemed very strange considering it was already the middle of the night, so the Oritas, who couldn't very well just sit there, got into the car and drove down the bumpy, ill-lit roads of the southern district to Mitsuko's house, only to find it looking dark and deserted. No matter how many times they called "Miss Kitamura!" there was no reply but, oddly, the door was unlocked, and when they opened it and went inside, turning on the lights, they found everything neatly put away, with a strange chill in the air, and then Mr. Orita gasped in surprise, pointing at a poster tied to a pillar in a spot where anyone coming through the garden could see it immediately, for written on it in big letters with a pink magic marker were the words "The Kitamura School is now closed."

The next day, the Oritas got a telegram from Mitsuko, saying: HAVE ESCAPED WITH FUKIKO STOP TAKE CARE. The house where Mitsuko had lived was soon torn down to make room for some apartments, and by the time construction began, the children were all going to new cram schools, and hardly ever ventured into that part of town again.

MISSING HEELS

$\mathcal{W}$hen the 9:17 arrived at Central Station that night, either the car or the platform must have been askew, because I lost my balance and fell flat on top of my suitcase, which had flown out ahead of me. I heard a man's voice from behind saying either, "I didn't push you," or "It wasn't me who pushed you." I thought I'd heard eggs cracking in the suitcase, which worried me, so I opened it and found all three of my hard-boiled eggs still intact, but since all I'd packed besides were some clothes, three thick notepads, and a fountain pen, I couldn't imagine where the sound had come from. Anyway, being pitched out onto the platform like that made me feel like a canvas mailbag, even after I'd stood up, brushed myself off, and straightened my hair. I looked up to see an enormous billboard looming over me, and a huge man in overalls peeling the old sign off with fingers far too delicate for someone of his bulk. As he tore away the stomach of a woman in blue tights, a breakfast eggcup and teapot appeared, then a whale off to one side, another layer down. When he'd peeled off as much as he could, the man took a bunch of neatly folded posters out of his bag, dipped his brush into a bucket of glue, painted the lower left-hand corner of the billboard, slapped on one of his new pictures, brushed the space next to it, unfolded another picture and pasted it on, then moved on to another part, unfolding and pasting as he went. I watched the nimble fingers as I've often done since childhood, until they seemed to be drawing me physically into them.

Suddenly, a man walking behind me snarled, "No use trying to hide that sort of thing. Everybody's going to notice." Startled, thinking he'd been talking to me, I looked around, but with crowds of people shuffling by it was impossible to tell where the voice had come from. The ceiling was as high as a church, so voices drifted up and reverberated in midair, mingling and circling overhead like the sound of wings. Staring up, the roof looked cockeyed, but when I looked down again I realized that the floor seemed slanted because everyone was stumbling forward as they walked, never glancing down, their eyes trained on some far-off spot. Gazing upward again, I saw that the entire building was a huge dome, ribbed like the inside of a whale, with butterflies, or tiny birds, or perhaps motes of dust glittering as they caught the light, floating in the air far above; but since watching them made me dizzy, I decided to keep my eyes on the platform, which wasn't much better because it still seemed to be on a slant, so in the end all I could do was stand there clutching my suitcase. The notepads in it were square, and bulky. Long ago, inspired by a childish daydream, I wrote a story about a trip around the world on the same kind of pad, but now that I was actually here in a strange land all the pages were blank, as if my own story had adopted me. Since no one in this city knew the slightest thing about me, the person I'd been until now might as well be dead, and that's how they would probably see me here—as a corpse with a smug-looking smile, or a newborn baby, humble but self-absorbed. The phrase "straight from the orchard" gives an impression of freshness, when in fact fruit that's just been torn off the tree is actually newly dead; a fresh cadaver, so to speak, which happened to be pretty much how I felt at the time. A redcap carrying two suitcases marched like a robot across my path, and when a new destination flashed on the electronic signboard, I hurried out into the city to keep myself from reading it.

The people and cars that had crowded the main road disappeared when I turned onto a side street, but there were some children squatting on the pavement grimly drawing chalk circles, and they burst out laughing the moment they saw me. I stood there a while looking into a line of mouths with gappy teeth, smelling sweat mingled with the sticky sweetness of fruit juice, then turned around to see a little girl crouching behind me, reaching for my heel. Pulling my foot away as though it hurt, I glared at her, which made her twist her face into an ugly frown; the others only laughed louder. I started to walk away, but stopped and looked back to see a boy now peering mischievously at my heel. "What do you want?!" I asked sharply, and immediately regretted having sounded like a tourist bawling out an overly persistent local hawking souvenirs. But the children didn't seem to understand and, in lieu of an answer, began singing a song that, as far as I could make out, went something like, "Ever see a squid try getting into bed? If you've got no heels, you don't know where to tread." That voice at the station came back to me: "No use trying to hide that sort of thing. Everybody's going to notice," and I anxiously clutched my suitcase. To the best of my knowledge, I didn't have anything to hide, but it dawned on me that there might be something wrong with me I didn't know about, and that perhaps that was why they were all laughing at me, which made me start to worry. Why, for instance, had there been no passport inspection or Customs at the station? Was it all part of some sinister plot? If anyone had wanted to know I would gladly have told them I was on my way to #17 Central Post Office Street, but no one had asked, which meant that nobody in town knew why I'd come and, in turn, that I could no longer tell if this undertaking of mine was just something I'd dreamed up or something tangible I could depend on. If it hadn't been for the papers in my pocket, I would have felt pretty lonely.

Since there was no one I could ask for directions, I had to first find the street on the map and then look for it ahead of me. It was a nuisance having to search for everything twice—once by reference and once by sight —but if that was the way things were done here that's how I would do them, and anyway, when there's no one around to help, you just have to work things out for yourself. I was used to crowds of people without a street, but this was the first time I'd seen a street with no people. Still, Central Post Office Street was easy enough to find. There was no sign of life at #17, though; all the curtains were drawn, and there was no answer when I rang the bell at the gate with two stone pillars on either side, pointed at the top like rockets. So I headed straight back to the station—not because I'd given up the idea of staying at #17—I intended to come back later. "Giving up" wasn't something I was used to, as I'd never actually had to *try* to enter a building to meet someone; I was always inside almost before I knew it, with whoever it was I'd wanted to meet right there in front of me, so I didn't know how to go about experiencing disappointment or failure. Besides, since there had always been someone I could count on to pay my way, I'd never got into the habit of carrying money around, so although it was hunger that drew me back to the station, I had nothing to buy food with, which was why I was hoping at least to find some place where they were handing out free samples; but apparently they didn't do that here, because the doors to the restaurants were all shut, with only typewritten menus tacked onto the windows, and no inviting smells wafting in the air. I looked closer and saw numbers on the menus, something like a timetable, which made me wonder if meals were served at set times in this country and the restaurants closed for the rest of the day. A fat white cat standing on the next corner stared at me as I approached, then abruptly made a right turn and hurried off down an alley, slipping between the garbage cans with a very light step for such a fat cat, and as I followed it I wondered whether cats had a specific target in mind when they set out or whether they just went where they pleased and came upon their prey accidentally, and yet in spite of not even knowing if they imagined their target (assuming they had one, that is) in words or pictures or smells, here I was trailing after this cat, perhaps because it seemed like an animal I could trust, so very sure of itself, whereas I had no target of my own at all.

I heard a woman with a beautiful face and a thick neck say, "When the guy who came to help me with my lessons seduced me and got me pregnant, I came over here for an abortion and never left," and another one say, "My kid's been down with the mumps since yesterday." At least that's what I thought they said. Both wore cardigans with the same pattern, so they may have been the same nationality, even though they didn't look alike. They were chatting in front of a street vendor's stall waiting for their food, but when they noticed me standing off to one side they stopped and turned around, apparently finding me (though not my heels) intriguing. The man behind the stall, peering out from time to time, throwing in an occasional comment, seemed to know them, and though he moved about too much for me to get a good look at him, I felt he was watching me and besides, the smell of whatever it was he was cooking drew me toward the stall, until I remem-

bered I didn't have any money and turned away, but
then he beckoned, the two women joining in, inviting me to come and eat with them. They seemed to
think it was me who couldn't understand, whereas it
was obviously the other way around, because when I
told them I didn't have any money there was no reaction, just the same gestures. When the man put a plate
of white meat floating in a thick black sauce in front of
me, they gestured so enthusiastically that I finally began
to slurp up the sauce, which tasted like ink at first but
was only slightly sour as it slid down my throat, and as
my stomach filled with warmth I suddenly noticed that
the stall was painted green and the sky was tinged with
yellow. They say that hunger dulls the vision and sharp-
ens the hearing, but I found the women's chatter harder
to catch on a full stomach, while every pimple and old
mosquito bite on their faces stood out clearly. To show
my gratitude, I went behind the stall to help the man,
who refused at first but finally consented, telling me to
tear off the ears of some squid. This looked simple but
was actually quite tricky, because if you yanked the ears
by the tip, the skin slipped off in your fingers, leaving
the bone behind, and if you grabbed them at the base
they were so stiff they wouldn't come off at all, but if you
fiddled around too long the flesh got warm and trans-

lucent and dissolved in your hands. Ripping the ears off all at once, which was clearly the best way, made a sound like silk tearing—actually more like a squid screaming, I thought, feeling slightly sick. I couldn't help wishing he stocked earless squid, but then maybe he wasn't from around here, and this troublesome variety was the only one available to him, or perhaps he had so little education that he believed it when people told him squid have ears, and so was duped into buying a kind that shouldn't even have existed. If he'd been a zoologist he could have officially registered this new species, the eared squid, giving it a Latinized version of his own name, but presumably here, as in any other country, people who actually shared their lives with animals not listed on any zoological charts were precisely the ones experts never let into their laboratories. Finding myself staring at the man's heels, I quickly turned back to my next squid and tugged with all my might, but the ears refused to budge. These mollusks, which swim along with their legs dangling out in front when they're hunting and dart off head-first when they need to escape, can go whichever way they please—up, down, right, left—on their ten heel-less legs. I rather liked the idea myself, of being able to go backward as easily as going forward, and was only discouraged by the thought that if I told anyone this, they would think I too had no heels. Eventually, when I'd ripped the ears off I don't know how many squid, the man said I'd better go home, so with my suitcase clasped to my chest, I went back to #17 Central Post Office Street. No one answered the bell this time, either, but after the third ring I saw the curtain on the window farthest to the left open a crack, and knew that someone must be peering out. I waved enthusiastically to let the man I'd be meeting for the first time know it was me, but the curtain closed and the door didn't open, so I took the papers out of my pocket and, not knowing whether he was watching or not, held them over my head. Nothing happened, so all I could do was open the gate, walk through the garden to the door, and sit down on the stone steps. I looked up at the plants—roses of some kind—and watched them tremble and sway until the sky behind them began to get dark, but no matter how long I waited it seemed night would never fall, which made me think I'd come to a place where the twilight was unusually long; but then I must have dozed off because when I awoke it was pitch-dark, and, to my surprise, the door was ajar. There was no one around. Inside was a dimly lit, well-polished wooden corridor, lined with doors on both sides, each one open a crack.

Leaving the front door wide open I went in, but stopped short when I heard the floor creak. I never make a sound when I walk, yet here, however careful I was, the wood squeaked, reminding me of a squid screaming. Oddly enough, though, remembering the man and his work at the stall made any fears I had vanish, and I started down the corridor, opening doors as I went. All the rooms had strange furniture of the sort you'd only see in the movies, with switches on the wall to turn on huge chandeliers overhead, but as for living things, however bright the light, I didn't even see a mouse, so I just kept going until I reached the end of the corridor, where I found a tiled kitchen by the staircase, which made me think of having something to eat before I went upstairs. Raiding the refrigerator in a strange house would be considered pretty outrageous in any country, but I was here legally, as an official mail-order bride, and even though I hadn't actually seen a husband, he had the ten photographs I'd sent, including some of me in a bathing suit, which made us practically old friends, so surely I had the right, being legally married to him, to consume whatever he had in the kitchen if I wanted to, and if he didn't like it, he could come out here himself and tell me about it. He was being pretty outrageous himself, hiding like this when he knew I was his wife. He certainly had no reason to be frightened, so perhaps he was playing games, or maybe he just wanted to surprise me; but with no way of knowing, I decided to ignore him for the time being and open the refrigerator, which, I discovered, was full of dairy products I wasn't familiar with: sour-tasting milk that poured like molasses, unsweetened yoghurt, white cheese, cheese with blue mold, cheese like grains of rice, and I ate and ate as though possessed, and soon stopped worrying about him. After all, he was only one part of this marriage; as long as I could live here, eat this lovely stuff every day, and go to school wherever I wanted, as the papers in my pocket promised, it didn't really matter what sort of man my husband was. Just as I'd put the last bit of cheese in my mouth, however, I turned around to see two eyeballs staring out at me from the crack in the kitchen door. When I went over to open it, the eyes disappeared, and their owner escaped down the hall. Though I'm no cat when it comes to chasing things, I chased him right up the stairs, but he dashed behind a black door and shut it from inside. I knocked on the door, and since I didn't know what people here shout in this sort of situation, all I could do was keep pounding, until my hand began to ache, at which point I decided that as I didn't really have to see him that day anyway I might as well just brush my teeth and go to bed. There was a bed in the room next to the black door, so I went in and opened the closet to find seventeen nightgowns, neatly arranged in order of size, with the largest on the left. The smallest fitted me perfectly, but whether my husband expected me to grow into the next one, or had no idea what size I took, or had divorced sixteen other women, all bigger than me, I couldn't imagine. In a corner of the room was a small basin with a single toothbrush, the same shade of peach as the nightgowns.

I woke up to find a teapot and cup on the bedside table, with steam rising from the pot, and a single bill under the cup. I was sure my husband had come in while I was asleep, because I remembered seeing him in a dream. Distressed about how old he was, he had both hands over his face so I could only see his eyes, which seem to be the only facial feature that doesn't really show one's age, but he was doubled over, gasping for breath, and each time he told me how much he envied me my youth I seemed to get a year younger, which was a surprisingly painful process. Aging is natural, but getting younger is like having something gnawing at your head, and when I protested through my tears, "Why did you put all those nightgowns in the closet?

They were bigger than me to begin with, and if I keep getting smaller and smaller like this, there won't be a single one I can wear," he was startled, perhaps unnerved to see how blunt I could be, for he laughed unnaturally loud, yet he must have been impressed all the same because he paid me a compliment, saying, "A smart cookie like you should go to the best school in town, starting tomorrow." Naturally enough, after having that dream, I was now keen to start school, but wasn't sure exactly how to start looking for one, and as I sipped my tea I noticed that rain was beating down on the stone path leading up to the front door, which meant I'd have to find an umbrella before I even started searching for a school, and it was my husband, if I could only catch hold of him, who would probably get me both, assuming—and there was no reason to doubt it, since he'd gone to the trouble of making me some tea—that he didn't regret having married me; so I got dressed and went and knocked on the black door, with no luck this time either, but while I was standing there I heard plates clinking downstairs. "That must be him fixing breakfast," I thought cheerfully, but when I ran downstairs there was no sign of him except for an empty egg stand by one of the two plates on the kitchen table, with tiny bits of shell scattered all around it.

When he peels his eggs, he breaks the shell into little pieces, I thought to myself, sitting down and taking a slice of neatly cut bread. My own hard-boiled eggs which I'd brought with me in the suitcase the other day had probably started to go bad by now. I remembered someone on the train telling me how people around here insisted on having their eggs served in an upright position, and that something called an "egg stand" had been devised for that purpose, so I must never, under any circumstances, eat an egg that was lying on its side, but seeing one of these devices actually sitting by my plate aroused my sense of mischief, for some reason, and, holding an egg sideways, pretending it was a globe, I cut the shell along the equator, split it into two equal halves, and took the contents out. I then put the two empty halves back in the stand, making it look like a normal egg. My husband would probably have told me I was being uncivilized, but since he didn't eat with me, he couldn't even see what I'd done, much less complain about it or try it himself.

I decided to use a little room next to the kitchen with a writing desk by the window because big rooms make me feel lonely, but no sooner was I inside it than I heard a noise again in the kitchen, followed by footsteps running upstairs, so I rushed back and found the doors to the dish cupboard next to the table half open, and not a single plate inside, which told me my husband must have been hiding in there, holding his breath while I was having breakfast, and that he'd just gone back upstairs, but even though I knew now what was going on I returned to the small room and didn't bother to chase after him. "If I don't write my mother soon she'll worry, but if I tell her the truth she'll be worried sick," I thought as I sat down, and ended up stringing together some starry-eyed lines about how kind my husband was, how big the house was, how plentiful the food and how pleasant the weather was, assuring her that all in all my married life had got off to a good start.

Posting a letter in Central Post Office Street shouldn't, one would have thought, present any problems, so I took mine and went out when the rain had let up, looking back as I passed through the gate, noticing that the curtains on a second-floor window were open a crack, thinking "My husband's watching," and feeling, unlike yesterday, almost as though this were natural. I walked down the wet path in the opposite direction from the way I'd come the day before. After a while I came to a building where a steady stream of people carrying envelopes were filing inside, so I joined them, but when I handed my letter in at the window, a clerk with pockets of sagging flesh at the sides of his mouth took out a ruler, measured the envelope, and shook his head in disbelief. He placed my letter on a scale, which he carefully examined, and, shaking his head again, gazed up at me in what might have been either anger or sympathy, I couldn't tell which, though it turned out that he was merely telling me how much I owed him, not how he felt about it. There seemed to be so many things I couldn't understand here, which made me all the more anxious to start school, so I got hold of a telephone directory and started looking up schools, and when I came across a name that appealed to me I picked up a ballpoint pen I noticed lying there on the counter and was about to write down the address when I saw what was printed along the side: "Taking even a single pen is stealing." I quickly put the pen back on the counter, memorized the address of the General Training School for Beginners, and left.

On my way there the rain started again, plastering my hair to my scalp and drenching the shoulders of my heavy jacket, and when I walked faster it caught me head-on, soaking my blouse so it stuck to my skin and you could see my breasts right through it. While I was hesitating at the door of the school it opened and a woman wearing glasses came out to ask what I was doing there, so I told her I'd come to find out about enrolling, and though I thought she gave my heels a quick glance I must have imagined it, for she put her arm around my shoulders and steered me inside, saying she couldn't really talk out there in the rain. The room she led me into had seven or eight depressing landscapes on the walls. Judging from the poise she showed in the way she moved her hands and eyes she may have been head of the school, but I caught a strong whiff of sleeping pills. It's quite wrong to think that tranquilizers have no smell; everything has its own smell, it's just that some people can't detect it. If this woman couldn't get to sleep at night, I thought, it probably wasn't due to money problems, and certainly wasn't a matter of age, which left the possibility that there was some disaster in the offing I alone didn't know about, something awful waiting to happen to this city.

"What do you want to learn?" she inquired, which seemed a strange question for a teacher to ask a prospective student. "I've no idea, that's why I need to go to school. I don't know anything about the people here," I replied. "What exactly do you want to find out about them?" she asked, and while I was trying to think what to say she added, "Don't be shy, now, I want you to tell me everything," insinuating that she knew things about me I myself was unaware of, but, unable to imagine what they were, I answered simply, "I'd like to start with everyday customs, I think," to which she promptly replied, "What kind of customs?" so I said the first thing that popped into my head: "Taking a bath, for instance, things like that," which seemed to suit her well enough. "OK, we'll start with that today," she said, then lowered her voice and added threateningly, "but this won't be the end of it, you know, because women like you are not only a social problem but a political problem as well." "Why is that?" I asked, but she dismissed my question, saying only, "I'll tell you in good time. Our topic for today is the bath," and, turning around, she took a painting off the wall behind her to reveal a small blackboard underneath. "Baths are normally taken after we rise, and before breakfast," she announced, writing the words "rise" and "breakfast" on the blackboard, which I found a bit surprising, so I asked, "Why clean yourself as soon as you get up? Is it because of dreams—because you get dirty wandering through the forest of your dreams?" but she didn't answer, and from the way she was staring at me I gathered I'd hurt her feelings, so perhaps the morning bath in her case was to wash off the smell of sleeping pills.

Whatever the reason, my husband must have found it strange that I hadn't taken a bath that morning. "The number of persons in the tub is usually limited to one," the woman went on, writing "one person" on the blackboard, and since she was now peering suspiciously into my eyes I blurted out, "Oh, I always have mine alone, too, except when I go to the public bath," at which she commented smugly, "Fortunately, we have no public baths here. That's why there are so few people suffering from skin disease."

Continuing the lecture, she explained: "The two methods of bathing are to shower, and to wash while sitting in the tub. The average length of time spent in the shower is two minutes and seventeen seconds," making me realize that if I wasn't careful my husband might think I'd drowned, seeing as I'm never out in less than an hour. "What are you thinking now?" the woman asked anxiously, so I answered, "Nothing really," to which she replied, "You're thinking everything I tell you is wrong, aren't you?" and when I shook my head she reversed the attack: "Well, then, how do you know it *isn't* wrong?" At a loss, I said in my defense, "But don't you see? Since I know so little anyhow, I've no choice but to believe what you tell me ... and why should it bother you, anyway? If it *does* happen to be wrong I'll find out sooner or later, so why start quizzing me now?" but, still not satisfied, she kept on at me: "You're thinking 'This teacher isn't really all that bright,' aren't you?" and it wasn't until I'd assured her, "I couldn't care less how smart people are. That sort of thing's never mattered to me," that the woman finally shut up. But whereas all I wanted was to learn more about bathing customs, this question of intelligence or stupidity was apparently of such concern to her that she finally burst into tears, accusing me of telling elaborate lies just to see if she could sniff them out. I was testing her, I must be a spy, sent by the headmaster. It was appalling, unthinkable—so this was how they went about selecting heads of department! As her troubled imagination rose to new heights of hysteria, her pores opened and the smell of sleeping pills grew stronger, so to shake off my own distress I gave her some advice on getting a good night's sleep: try breaking her routine and, before going to bed, soak in a lukewarm tub for seventeen minutes. This ended the class, though I found myself reconstructing it all in my head on the way home, despite having no one to talk to about what had happened that day.

Although the house was silent, the lights were on and there was some white, creamy soup in a pan on the stove, but since having everything done for me this way was more like living in a hotel than being married, I made up my mind in bed that night to start cooking like a real wife the next day, and then slid pleasantly into sleep. In the dream I had, my husband was much older than he'd been the night before but tonight that didn't seem to bother him, and since his smiling face somehow reminded me of my grandmother I took the initiative, putting my arms around his neck, stroking his wet hair and shirt, squeezing the artificial hand that hung there limp, guiding it along the contours of my body, feeling it become warmer and start moving on its own, realizing, finally, that this was a dream but holding my breath so I wouldn't make a sound, moving as little as possible to keep from waking up, it was such a *good* dream, until my husband let out a deep sigh and stood up, saying, "This may be fun for you but for me it's all work," and tried to fold me up and put me in a suitcase, which upset me so much I kicked him, my foot hitting him square on the chin, knocking him flat on his back, but when I hurried to help him he jumped up on his own and ran away. I knew I was awake when I looked over and saw the same tea set and money on the bed-side table. Where yesterday there'd been one bill, today there were two. When I went to the kitchen the first thing I did, of course, was to open the cupboard door, but this morning it was full of neatly stacked dishes, without a trace of anything you could call a husband, and not a sound, either, to show whether he was in the room behind the black door or had gone out, so when I saw the fragments of eggshell he'd left on the table again, I picked them up in my fingers, tossed them lightly into my mouth, and ate them. If, I wondered, I told him, "In *my* country we eat the shells and throw the eggs away—after all, the shell's full of calcium, which makes your fingernails strong, but all you get from the egg is a lot of cholesterol," would he get angry and say, "You're testing me—telling lies to see if I can sniff them out," or say, "You think I'm dumber than I look, don't you?" and burst into tears? Thanks to my first day of school I could imagine having this sort of conversation with him, so the thought of going back today made me sit up straight in anticipation, but before I left I washed the breakfast dishes, wiped the table, and made my bed like a proper housewife. The road to school passed through a residential area with no stores and no one on the street, so I wasn't likely to learn much about life in the city unless I went out of my way and ventured into the shopping district, but, wanting to avoid crowds of people who might stare at my feet, I decided to head straight for school. I arrived to find the same teacher standing in front of the door, smoking a cigarette in a desperate sort of way, sucking at the filter as though if she didn't get it in her mouth fast enough it would escape, inhaling greedily, determined that the smoke should permeate every nook and cranny of her body, then snorting it out in disgust, equally determined to blow all the poison out. Watching her brought back that sense of impending doom, reinforcing the feeling that this city was living out its last moments in the shadow of some imminent crisis. "You were going to tell me smoking's bad for my health, were you? Well, I know that," she laughed scornfully, dropping the cigarette butt and crushing it with the toe of her shoe. There must have been a reason for stamping out with such hatred something that had been in her mouth a moment before, but I didn't know how to broach the subject, so when she asked, "And what do you want to learn today?" all I said was, "Could you please teach me what to do when I go shopping?" which didn't interest me in the least, though she seemed relieved to hear this request. "On entering a shop, the first thing you do is say 'Hello,'" she explained. "You never have? Well, then, it's a good thing I told you, because if you didn't know, you might be taken for a thief." "And when you leave the shop, do you say 'Goodbye'?" I asked as a joke, but the teacher nodded so gravely I got the giggles and went into a spasm of coughing, which she calmly waited out before continuing pedantically: "Omitting the proper words of parting is bad. It's only natural you should say 'Goodbye'; it's the bare minimum. Furthermore, since you say it just before you leave—and however heartfelt you make it—there's no danger of being caught up in a long conversation afterward, so it's worth taking some trouble over." By implication, though a marriage might take no time at all, a divorce should be stretched out forever; if I were to separate from my husband, I'd have to spend plenty of time doing it. When I then asked if she'd taken a bath last night before going to bed, seeing as she didn't reek of sleeping pills today, she was silent a moment before scolding: "You mustn't change the subject with no warning like that. You're not a child," which annoyed me, so I told her, "What's wrong with changing the subject? If even children can do it, then why not adults?" but she just smiled and said, "I'm sorry, I shouldn't have said children when it's actually people with no education who keep shifting from one topic to the next." That really put my back up, and I couldn't help saying, "Well, if an education makes people so dumb they can't follow a conversation unless they stick to the same topic, then you're better off without one, aren't you?" but she kept that smile plastered on her face and continued, "Education or the lack of it is a problem of class, not of the individual. You can tell when people belong to the same class by the way they talk; they make an effort to dress alike and read the same magazines; they keep an eye on each other to make sure everyone can tell who they are at a glance. It's the same with the way we speak, though I doubt whether you can tell yet." Just then the door opened and a young man, probably another student, walked in and, without a trace of embarrassment, or confusion, or emotion of any kind at seeing me there, shoved his hands in his pockets and said, "I guess I'm early." I felt hostile for the first time since arriving in the city, but when I tried to hide it by smiling sweetly and saying hello he continued to ignore me, turning instead to the teacher and announcing bluntly, "That brooch is nice," at which she smiled vaguely, caught off guard, and although I was a bit ashamed of not having noticed the brooch myself, the boy's skin, smooth as a freshly picked peach, made me angrier still, so finally I pushed my chair back noisily and stood up.

"I'll be back tomorrow," I said before dashing outside, where I kept on running in the opposite direction from home. The houses grew smaller and grayer and older, with broken windows and crumbling concrete facades, and thin-legged children squatting down playing in the street who didn't even look up as I passed by. When a little girl's eyes happened to meet mine, she said, "There's a festival down by the port today. There'll be fireworks at ten," but her face was so blank and the voice so utterly devoid of emotion I couldn't tell whether she was urging me to go because it would be fun, or warning me to avoid it and go straight home, or simply pleased with herself for knowing about it. Further down the road I found a familiar smell wafting by my nose, luring me into a restaurant with a sign so old and rusty I couldn't read it. In the dim light some skinny men with heavy beards were sitting at the counter playing cards, muttering over their bets. A woman's piercing voice asked if I wanted a meal; there may have been no menu there, for she stared at me expectantly, and while she waited with great patience and goodwill for me to name one of her set dishes, I was still trying to remember that smell, thinking that what I really wanted was a list of aromas rather than names of dishes, but when I sniffed the air to show her what I meant, she nodded at once and disappeared into the kitchen. Seeing the woman's bare feet, stuck in a pair of sandals, I wondered why she didn't wear boots or something to hide her heels, but I was literally worrying over nothing, because a person with heels to hide has no need to hide a lack of them, and besides, there's no such thing as a human being without heels anyway. If there *were* such people they would form their own social class, immediately recognizable by the way they talked and the magazines they read, making it pointless to hide their feet. Before the word "class" could make me angry again, however, I heard a noise and looked out the window to see some boys run by, setting off firecrackers. As if to draw my attention away from the sight, a large plate now appeared in front of me with a mountain of garlic salad in the middle. "Ah! So that's what that smell was," I thought, relieved that the memory had finally come back. The smell was so strong I wanted to hold my nose, but my recent diet of cheese and other dairy products had left me longing for hotter, more pungent fare, so I cheerfully set to work, soon breaking into a sweat, until I suddenly realized I'd forgotten the required greeting on entering a shop, and turned to the men playing cards and shouted "HELLO!" to which all seven of them responded by turning around in unison and, without cracking a smile, placing their cards on the counter and walking slowly toward me. One by one they stuck out their hands for me to shake. They were tiny hands for such big men, and I wondered if my husband's were this small, or if theirs had shrunk from too much card playing, but my husband wasn't a foreigner, nor did he hang around in restaurants, so he must have big, white hands. It was dark now, with the streetlamps shining softly through the mist and more and more firecrackers going off outside, so I asked the way to the port, paid the bill, and left the restaurant, turning down the dark alley by the Fishermen's Union Warehouse and heading due south, just as I'd been told. A man in a suit, who apparently couldn't bear the thought of me overtaking him, glared at me and quickened his pace until he was gasping for breath, but just as we were passing the Warehouse Entrance for Large Vehicles we heard voices coming from behind a truck, followed by an explosion at the man's feet, which made him scream in a high, woman's voice, bringing hoots of laughter from the shadows. "Knock it off and come on out here!" he shouted, in a decidedly masculine voice this time, and three boys in black jackets shuffled out, sneering and swaggering. Making it sound as insulting as he could, the man said "Foreigners, eh?..." at which the tallest of them stepped silently away from his mates, lunged forward, and kicked him in the stomach. He groaned and doubled over, staggering along clutching his stomach with one hand and holding himself up with the other, yet even so he managed to say, "I'll call the police!" and it was only after he started saying "And when they get hold of the likes of you ..." that the same boy kicked him from behind, laying him flat out on the pavement, chin first. Without a beard to protect it, the skin must have peeled right off. The boy then turned to me. When I realized he was asking if the man at his feet was a customer of mine I quickly shook my head, and after watching the three walk away I went over and knelt down beside him.

"Are you all right?" I asked, but he just gave me a dirty look and told me if I was that creep's sister, reform school was where he belonged, the sooner the better. I spat in his face, then took off for the port without pausing to look back, racing past fur coats and down jackets until I saw water, and when I finally reached the edge of the dark sea, shimmering with lights from the boats, I stopped to catch my breath. The clock on the pier said it was still only nine o'clock. A cheerful hubbub of voices came from a bar right in front of me, and propelled by loneliness and boredom and anxiety I went in to find the air swirling with excitement, making my ears ring, yet not a face in sight, just a solid mass of backs, jostling and heaving, but since everyone here apparently preferred to drink standing up, there was an empty stool at the bar that might almost have been reserved for me. As soon as I sat down, or rather climbed up onto it, I was caught up in what was going on behind the counter. The woman who ran the place was in constant motion, with about thirty checks spread out in front of her like a deck of cards, and as the customers called out their orders she'd jot them down, managing at the same time to pour beer, open soft drinks, wash empty beer mugs and line them up on a shelf, without pausing for a moment. The boy behind the counter had a lovely long neck and eyelashes like a lama's but seemed a little slow, for when the woman asked him sweetly to fetch a glass for her, although he didn't grumble you couldn't say he snapped to it, either, just ambling over to the cupboard and then returning without the glass, murmuring wistfully, "God, I'm hungry." She could have been sharp with him, but quickly made him a sandwich instead, which he took with a smile, his cheeks puffed out in anticipation, and by the time he asked, "Can I eat it here?" she was already back at the cash register. "Sure," she said without looking up, her voice quiet enough to cut through the din.

"Where's my beer?" shouted a gruff voice.

"Just a minute," the woman answered, handing the mug to the man next to me who took it without a word and delivered it, like a regular, to the waiting customer.

"Heard it was a white whale. Somebody found it when they were taking a walk," said someone behind me.

"A whale? In this filthy water?" The voice sounded familiar, so I turned around, but it was some man with a beer gut whom I'd never seen before.

"I'd like to order something, too." This came from a young man with a suntan and a brightly colored scarf around his neck, edging his way up to the side of the counter. He had a wheedling sort of voice.

"What'll it be?" she asked, and he named some impossible-sounding cocktails like "Pearl under the Palms" or "Pacific Rose."

"Don't do them," she said, brusquely this time.

"Then how about something to eat?"

"Don't do that either." Smothered laughter spilled out of the crowd, and with the fireworks fast approaching, the tension heightened. Still leaning on the counter, showing no signs of leaving, the man with the gaudy scarf asked, "Do you by any chance have a phone here?" to which the woman, without looking up from the glasses she was washing, answered, "No, we don't.

You won't find anything you're looking for here." "What do you mean by that?" he shouted angrily, craning forward over the bar, but when she looked up and he saw that he hadn't made her angry or upset, he calmed down, saying, "Well then, I guess I'll just have a beer." This, for reasons of his own, he offered to the lama-boy, who had finished his sandwich and was now asking for something to drink, but when the boy backed away with a worried look he got miffed and shouted, "Here! I said I'd give it to you, didn't I?" The boy, though, kept his distance.

Since the customers were now filing out the door, it was obviously time for the fireworks to start, so I followed them, coming face to face with the dark water again. Just then I felt someone's hand under my armpit, and turned to see a policeman in uniform. "It couldn't have been my brother who kicked that man in the suit—I don't even have one," I told him. "I mean, that boy may have a sister, but it's not me." When my attempt to defend myself met with silence, I figured that wasn't what he was arresting me for, so I changed my tack, pleading, "Can't you at least wait till the fireworks are over? I haven't seen any in your city yet," but, still without a word, he led me away. Not knowing where he was taking me, I blurted out, "Wait," remembering something else, "if this is about Customs it's not that I lied or anything. There were no Customs booths at the station; in fact, I didn't even see us cross any border, and besides, I didn't have anything to declare," but to no avail. Before long, the roofs started to look familiar and I realized he'd brought me back to Central Post Office Street, and when we reached #17 he opened the gate and went right in through the front door as though he owned the place, then took me upstairs, threw me down on the bed and left the room. I was surprised to hear a knock nearby, followed by the sound of a door opening, so I jumped up and ran to look, but the black door was already shut, leaving me to stand there listening to the two of them (though, to tell the truth, since I'd never heard either man speak I wasn't really sure if it was the policeman and my husband or not). Even with my ear to the door all I could pick out were odd words like "charge" and "loss," so not only was it impossible to follow, I couldn't even tell from the tone of their voices whether they were having a serious discussion or an argument or simply a conversation. After a while, I gave up and went back to my room, where I brushed my teeth and put on my nightgown, then closed my eyes to watch the fireworks I'd missed explode behind my eyelids, the glowing sparks floating slowly, reluctantly down, stinging me as they touched my elbows and knees, and when the display was over, my body grew dull and heavy, then soft and pliant, and in my dream that night my husband was the lama-boy from the bar. I'd always wanted a husband like this, but convention had made me think I had to marry a man with a good education, who could make money, who was older and more experienced, and when I showed a natural preference for bashful boys, soft as marshmallows and much younger than me, I was met with a chorus of "How could you!" "You ought to be ashamed!" "FORGET IT!" and so had been losing out all these years. The boy tried hard to please me, first rubbing his earlobes until his ears were pointed like horns, and when I laughed and said, "No, not there," he switched to his big toe, continuing to massage it even when it had swelled up like a balloon, which made me laugh so hard I could hardly breathe, but when I told him again, "No, not there, silly," he didn't understand and started scouring his belly button with his finger, which naturally did nothing but produce a smell of sesame in the air, while I just watched him patiently, imagining the fun I'd have picking out pants and sweaters that would look good on him. But wasn't he a bit on the thin side? I didn't like thin men, so I'd have to fatten him up with plenty of rich food, but would I be able to pay for it? And at the thought of money, I woke up.

I was annoyed with myself for not waking up at the sound of my husband's footsteps, or other signs of his presence, during the night. When I opened my eyes, though, the tea set was on the bedside table as usual, along with *three* bills; and I thought, "Some day, if I keep getting more and more money, I won't be able to manage without a lot of it," which worried me, but I was married now, so it couldn't be helped. On leaving the room I noticed the smell of rotten eggs, which I knew must be the ones I'd brought in my suitcase—but where was that suitcase? The smell came from the black door, so my husband must be storing the suitcase and the eggs inside it in there, or perhaps it was my notebooks he was keeping instead, but since I had nothing to record in them for the time being and didn't have time to write anyway, I decided to forget about it and went downstairs, to find no breakfast waiting, which meant I'd have to fix something for myself like a good housewife, which was exactly what I'd resolved to do the day before, I thought, as I took two eggs out of the refrigerator and put them in a pan of water. It occurred to me that my husband might actually be very young, a mere child who, after losing his wealthy parents, had been driven by loneliness to choose a bride by mail-order but wasn't old enough to marry her yet, and was hiding until he reached maturity. The floor of the room behind the black door might be covered with stuffed animals and Lego blocks, with a boy sitting in the middle of it looking at picture books, carefully studying the shapes of the letters, looking forward to the day when he'd be able to read lots of books so he could show off his knowledge to his wife.

The thought of school reminded me of that student, which was depressing, particularly when I recognized that I might be jealous of him, as the very idea of envying a perfect stranger who meant nothing to me was offensive, so I decided to go anyway, if only to prove to myself that I wasn't jealous. I suppose I may have wanted to get there before he did, for as I walked my pace kept getting faster and faster, until I arrived to find a thin woman I'd never seen before standing in front of the door.

"Where's my teacher?" I asked.

"Her maternity leave starts today, so I'll be teaching you in her place," she said, examining me carefully from the neck down and then asking "How far have you progressed in your studies?" which, to an outsider, might have suggested a course of some kind, on different levels, like a staircase, and which may have been the impression she wanted me to have.

Unwilling to play along, I said flippantly: "I'll always be a beginner—don't underestimate me."

"Oh? And does that mean you forget everything you're taught?" she inquired testily.

"No, it means that every time I learn something new a bit of old knowledge disappears, so my head keeps getting emptier and emptier, and there's plenty of room for new thoughts to grow."

"But your husband has a very different opinion concerning education, doesn't he?"

She'd touched a sore spot, but I answered quickly, the words rolling off my tongue: "Yes, that's right, he's interested in everything, he reads a lot and has this store of knowledge, putting his own ideas together like the pieces in a stained glass window."

As we entered the classroom, side by side, she lit a cigarette, saying she'd started smoking again since her divorce three months earlier, then asking, "Do you think *you'll* get a divorce?" looking so hopeful that I said, "Well, actually, we are having problems," letting the lie slip out before I knew it. Now that I think of it, this may have been the moment when I first learned that while telling someone your marriage is on the rocks may not earn you respect, it can at least gain you recognition as an adult. In any case, she told me she'd got divorced because her husband never wanted to go out, while she couldn't bear to stay in, so they spent all their holidays fighting and finally decided to split up, and when I commented without thinking, "My husband doesn't like to go out either, but it doesn't bother me enough to want a divorce," the woman glowered at me and said, "If it was just a question of him not wanting to go out it wouldn't have bothered me, either. The trouble was that every day he used to say, 'It beats me why you like to go out so much,' until it got so I was actually doing as he said: I went out every day, even when I didn't want to, even when my ankles were swollen; I'd go walking in the north wind with raw cheeks and frostbitten ears; for no earthly reason I'd wander weeping through the streets, enslaved by this 'love-to-go-out' personality that I'd somehow developed. I suffered until divorce finally liberated me." Listening to this made me realize how lucky I was, for my husband's personality wasn't fixed, so I could change it every day if I wanted to, within the bounds of my imagination, nor was I under any obligation to choose a definite personality for myself, and I was just thinking that this was the kind of marriage I wouldn't mind having a go at again when the teacher, after re-examining my clothes, broke in to inform me that recently women of an inferior sort were being brought into the country from poorer parts of the world, and since far too many of the men here were interested in them, marriage opportunities for her more liberated countrywomen were becoming more and more limited. She sat there, waiting for my reaction.

"I didn't know that," I replied.

"These are people who marry only for money," she went on, "who come from poor villages, and get divorced and go back to them when they've saved up enough. They're uneducated, which makes it extremely difficult to teach them what living as man and wife really means, but it was the sheer difficulty of the task that led me," she concluded proudly, "to choose teaching as my profession."

"But I'm not like those women," I declared. "I gave this decision a lot of thought, and came here of my own free will."

"Poor people have no will of their own," she said in a scathing tone of voice. "Whatever they do, they have no choice in the matter—poverty drives them to it." Having spoken her mind she sat, perhaps in anticipation of a counterattack, with her hands in lightly gripped fists and her chin thrust slightly forward, waiting for an answer.

Although I'd never made up my mind about anything before, this marriage had definitely been my own decision, so being told that poor people have no choice in anything was more than I could stand. "What do you know about someone you're meeting for the first time?" I fired back.

"If you steer the conversation in the right way you can find out everything about a person's life in the first five minutes. If this weren't true we wouldn't have therapists, would we? I used to be one myself, you know." Her brain was running smoothly now, like a well-oiled machine.

"But I'm not sick, so a therapist wouldn't be able to find out anything much about me. And anyway, since you're the one who's suffering, not me, maybe I should become a teacher so I can save you." She *was* suffering, all right—I could tell by the way her eyes twitched at the corners and her cheeks sagged, and most of all by the greasy smell in the air, but I couldn't figure out why, because that kind of sickly clamminess almost always appears when a person is struggling to catch up with something that's already too far ahead, yet as far as I could see this woman hadn't fallen behind anything—

and yet she reeked of it. Being told she was suffering didn't upset her at all, though; in fact, she was so pleased you might have thought this was evidence of her self-proclaimed powers of insight, and when she confessed she'd never met anyone who suffered as much as she did, I seized this opportunity for revenge and said, "Well, then, you didn't choose your profession, did you? Everything you've done so far has been because you had no choice—your suffering drove you to it. Suffering people can't make decisions, or even think for themselves." Feeling triumphant, filled with a sense of sadistic pleasure that shocked even me, I quickly assumed a humble attitude and added, "But let's not worry about that now. Do please go on teaching me about this city," to which she replied, "Why, there's nothing to teach—nothing out of the ordinary here. We're all leading quite normal lives." When I protested, "What do you mean 'normal'? I've yet to see anything I'd call 'normal' since I arrived," she stared at me in amazement.

I had been planning to go home and do some "cleaning" like a good housewife that day, but the house was so big I didn't know whether to start from inside or out, or whether to wash the windows and then scrub the floor or vice versa, and since there was no one to tell me I began in a vague sort of way with the kitchen, but the floor didn't get any cleaner no matter how hard I scrubbed since it wasn't really all that dirty in the first place, and while the hall wasn't exactly sparkling no amount of mopping made it any shinier, which meant that all this drudgery was just making my shoulders ache, so I tried washing the tablecloth, which bored me stiff and left me wondering exactly what I was trying to achieve through all this housework, but then I began to think that maybe the only really dirty thing in the house was my own body, for, after all, I'd been seeing a man I didn't know night after night, so I decided to take a bath. The bathroom was even bigger than you'd expect for a house like this—so huge that sitting in the tub all alone out there in the middle I felt as though I were floating in a little boat on the ocean; if the rug had been blue instead of green this could have been a sea voyage, and as I stared across that open space I had a sense of being watched, of a crowd of people watching me with puzzled eyes, for here I was soaking in a hot tub that was drifting on the sea—water in water—and they couldn't fathom what this "double bath" was all about. But whether my husband was among this teeming crowd I couldn't tell, they all looked alike, each one as wet as the next, all tangled up together like squid, so he could have been any one of them, I thought, relieved to know I didn't have to pick him out. Then I stood up and the sea disappeared, and I noticed that the door across the room was open a tiny crack. It was pitch dark on the other side of the door, so I couldn't see a thing. The room, by contrast, was far too bright. Covering myself with a towel I went to open the door, but, just as I'd expected, there was only the sound of escaping footsteps, and I was left there watching the water drip off me onto the floor. I'd lost weight, not for lack of food but because there was no one to eat it with, and if I didn't get my appetite back somehow I'd soon be suffering from malnutrition. There's an old saying that in a strange land it's easy to eat but hard to sleep, but my case was just the opposite— while I had no trouble sleeping, eating was another matter. Though I hadn't had a bite since breakfast I wasn't the least bit hungry, just terribly drowsy.

In my dream that night, for the first time I felt so depressed that when my husband came I wanted to turn away, yet not wishing to seem coldhearted I re-lented and put out my hands to make it at least look as if I was ready to catch him when he fell, but he seemed caught in midair, as though in a spider's web, with his arms flailing. I lay there watching, not even trying to help, thinking how phony it looked, like a performance put on to get my sympathy, when I noticed that tonight he was neither an old man nor a boy but in the prime of life, just the right age for a husband. His cheeks, though, glowed red from too much drink, which I didn't like at all, but I repressed the urge to slap him and started to say something nice and encouraging, yet somehow it came out wrong and I heard myself ask, "How many bills do I get today?" Brushing the cobwebs off the shoulder of his suit, he said, "Here," holding out five, but when I tried to tell him honestly that he'd given me one too many, since this was only my fourth day on the job, I lost my voice and my hand darted out instead, snatching the bills and shoving them in my pocket. That's the kind of person I am, I told myself—can't save a penny, always spend the lot, so I'll never be able to get divorced.

"What are you thinking about?" my husband asked, but my voice caught in my throat. "Something obscene, I hope. That'd suit me fine," he leered, but when I still didn't answer he had a fit and screamed, "What's the matter? You deaf or something?" and stuck a fountain pen in my ear, sending a stream of black ink seeping through my eardrum to invade my body. "With this ink in you you'll be just like me," he declared, and I was in the middle of saying, "What do you mean? You're no ink pot. So stop talking nonsense and give me back my notebooks," when I woke up. There were only four bills on the bedside table and my ears were dry on the inside, so it had been a dream, after all, and although there was no tea, it didn't necessarily mean my husband's feelings for me had cooled—I could easily boil some water myself.

When I went to the kitchen, there was a postcard at the bottom of the pan I boiled my eggs in, apparently confirming a hospital appointment, the date today, and the patient myself. This my husband must have arranged, and I was glad he'd done it, for although there was nothing strictly wrong with me the change in climate might have made me ill without my noticing it, and I didn't really want to go to school anyway, and when I looked out the window the sky was cloudy and gray— perfect hospital weather. True, I wasn't exactly at death's door, but I could think of lots of little symptoms: loss of appetite and occasional stomach cramps, for instance, plus a heavy feeling in the intestines after eating; pains in the knees when I went upstairs, and sore eyes when I stared into the darkness. As I stood waiting for the bus, recalling these complaints in detail, a tall woman dressed in the height of fashion approached, walking very fast in spike heels that made her seem about to stumble forward, her body pulled in all directions—hips up, chest forward, shoulders thrown back—so that she appeared to fill up more space with every step she took. She stopped in front of me and checked the bus schedule and then her watch, which she apparently didn't trust, because she then asked me the time, and when I replied, "You know, I'm not really sure," I noticed her peering at my feet.

The bus passed rows of houses that gradually became fewer and farther between, until finally, at the end of a sparse grove of withered trees, it stopped on top of a hill in front of the general hospital. I'd expected something more frightening, like a gothic castle, but the building resembled a school, gray and unassuming enough to give even someone like me who was here for the first time the feeling of knowing it quite well. When I handed the postcard to the nurse at the reception window, she read it and, shaking her head in disbelief, opened a huge file to look for something, then, shaking her head again when she found it, gave me my ticket—a wooden slat with the number 17 on it—and pointed to the right. Clutching my ticket, I walked in that direction, straight into a waiting room that looked like a hotel lobby. A little boy was lying fast asleep across the thighs of his short, stocky mother, and a long-limbed woman with a suntan sitting next to her looked up from the magazine she'd been reading to gaze at me, then set it down on the table to reveal a picture of a woman fishing in her bathing suit, which intrigued me for a number of reasons, but she apparently found me more interesting.

"It must be lonely coming to the hospital all by yourself."

"My husband's busy today," I lied.

Suddenly very polite, she asked, "Oh, so you're married?" then adding as though she didn't quite believe me, "And what does your husband do?" I was trying to figure out why anyone should be interested in what a perfect stranger did for a living when she asked, "Does he work in a factory?" to which I lied again, "No, he's in stocks and bonds," whereupon, looking satisfied, she cocked her head to examine my face from an angle and said, "I see, you're one of those mail-order brides, aren't you?"

"And what does your husband do?" I asked, parroting the question though I couldn't have cared less.

"My ex-husband was a manager but I now live alone," she answered. "You probably won't understand, but here in the city people are beginning to recognize the value of the single woman. It might seem lonely to you, but it isn't, as long as you have a profession," she concluded, having decided that I hadn't got one, and pitying me for it.

"May I ask what yours is?" I asked.

"I am an accountant," she answered proudly, and although that didn't tell me exactly what she did, I was beginning to see that if you wanted to be accepted socially it wasn't enough to be divorced, you needed a profession, too. The woman then began to tell me about the trouble she was having with her legs, which had been swelling up recently, but although they'd be so bad she couldn't leave the house on days when she wanted to go to work, or meet a friend, or pay a call on her sick mother, whenever she had a hospital appointment they shrank down to normal size, "like this," she said, lifting her skirt to her thighs to show me her thin, bony shanks.

"Exactly where is the swelling?" I asked.

"Around my heels," she answered emphatically, which made me uncomfortable, so I lied again.

"That happens to me a lot, too."

Refusing to believe me, the woman sat bolt upright and declared, "That can't be. No one's legs swell up and hurt the way mine do." Convinced that her particular symptoms were what distinguished her body from everyone else's, she insisted that I couldn't possibly be having the same trouble with my legs as she had with hers. Her efforts to claim sole possession of her physical condition through the uniqueness of "this swelling here," which no one else had ever seen, and "this pain here," unknowable to all but her, made the urge to poke fun at her irresistible.

"Oh, come on, I bet it doesn't hurt all that much," I teased, which, just as I'd expected, made her fly into a rage.

"What can a person like you who's never been sick know about pain?"

"But I do get sick," I replied, my own hackles rising. "My being here at the hospital is proof of that!"

"Oh, I know why you're here," she said scornfully, "—to get rid of a child, I imagine." Just at this point, the little boy who'd been sleeping on his mother's fat knees sat up and whimpered something like, "Mommy, you didn't come here to get rid of me, did you?" In lieu of an answer, the mother glowered at me in indignation, while the boy also turned to me and frowned, then took a toy pistol out of his pocket and marched toward me. I've always found children frightening, so I got up to take refuge by the window, but as I stood there gazing out, thinking I'd finally escaped the need to carefully navigate my way through this tiresome conversation, the long-legged woman rose and, picking up the magazine she'd set aside earlier, came over to show me the picture of the woman fishing.

"Is this what you and your husband do in your spare time?" she asked condescendingly. Realizing that this must be some hidden allegory or some idiom I didn't know, and that she was waiting for a chance to laugh at me for not knowing it, I told her, "No, my husband doesn't care for this sort of thing, and besides, when it's fish they're catching, why should people have to wear bathing suits in case they get wet?" at which the woman curled her lip again, and handed me a riddle: "Ah, but are swimsuits only for swimming?"

"Maybe a photograph of a trout in a bathing suit fishing for women would have been better," I said, trying to laugh it off, but she immediately shot back, "I see you're a realist, too," giving me further proof of how difficult it was to keep up a conversation one didn't really understand anyway. If the woman hadn't heard her number called and disappeared into an examining room just then, I don't know how I would have managed after that.

When my number was called I went inside to find a

large bearded man in a white coat standing there, staring sternly down at me like a temple guard. With a jerk of his chin he ordered me to sit on a stool. Plunking himself down in a massive armchair, he barked:

"Fever?"

"No."

"Headache? Backache?"

"No," I answered, and since the silence was getting awkward I added, "My body feels heavy, though."

"That means you're pregnant. Let's have a look," he said abruptly, grabbing a pair of tweezers and peering inside my ear. Calling for a flashlight, he began probing for something, but the more intently he searched the more embarrassed I felt, until I had to explain, "That black stuff isn't ear wax. My husband spilled some ink in my ear."

"Is he a novelist?" he asked, and before I knew it, a new lie had popped out. "No, he's an executive in an ink company." I was puzzled why everyone was so interested in my husband's occupation. It seemed that was all they cared about, and I didn't matter at all. "Ah!" the doctor cried, yanking my earlobe so hard I yelled, "That hurts!" at which he let go of it and muttered disappointedly, "So I was just imagining it," leaving me to rub my aching ear, resenting him for having nearly ripped it off.

"OK, lie down on the table," he ordered, but when I started to strip he stopped me and told me to take my socks off, which made my cheeks burn, and left me wondering whether I was supposed to take them off and then lie down, or lie down and then take them off, but since standing up was impossible, and lying down would have been odd, I finally perched on the edge of the table and almost had them off when three young nurses entered and started giggling the moment they saw me. After smoothing his hair down with a comb he'd taken from the pocket of his white coat, the doctor put some gloves on and started examining my feet. He was probing again, sliding his stethoscope slowly across my soles, but this time I was completely relaxed, for the body lying there on the table seemed to be someone else's, in no need of my help because not only was it quite capable of looking after itself, I even felt it would watch out for me if need be. Of this I was sure, for while "I" could have died of embarrassment when the nurses whispered and giggled, "the body" was perfectly at ease, neither wanting to be better than anyone else, nor resenting ridicule—that sort of thing simply didn't matter to it. And when the doctor said, "This part of the foot ought to be reinforced with plastic," it was the body's voice that answered calmly, "No, there's absolutely no need for that." Even before I understood why it wouldn't be necessary, I knew that this was my feeling as well.

"But you can't just leave it. Part of it's missing."

Without even flinching at the doctor's mechanical tone I asked, "What do you mean, 'missing'?" which set the nurses off again, prompting the doctor to turn to them and say, in a quiet voice that might have been either serious or sarcastic, "This is a lot of fun, isn't it?" as he ran the comb through his hair again. "Anyway, you can't go around with some of your foot missing, but if you're going to be difficult about it, you'll just have to see the head nurse in No. 17. I can't waste any more of my time," he ended and, with another jerk of his chin, ordered me off the table.

Hemmed in on three sides by bookcases, with a desk by the window piled too high with papers to let much light in, the room was deep in shadow, and the head nurse, who turned around when she heard me knock, had the vague aura of a photograph taken in the last century, sitting there frozen with a rubber stamp in her hand. When I went in and closed the door, the restless stir outside vanished, leaving only the ticking of the old-fashioned wall clock to mark the passage of time; the head nurse, having put down her stamp and

swiveled around to face me, was once again as motionless as a picture. Perhaps it was the barrier of tension
around her, created by her determination not to lose a
single moment as she struggled to keep from drowning
in waves of miscellaneous tasks, that made me blurt out,
"Sorry to bother you when you're so busy," and then,
immediately realizing that even this was a waste of time,
quickly add, "I'll only be a minute," another useless
comment, but the head nurse must have known that
simply waiting for me to state my business was the best
way to save both time and effort, for she neither protested nor pressed me to go on, although I've always had
trouble starting a conversation and found her silence
daunting, which made me awkward anyway.

"Actually, I was told to come and talk to you about
an operation on my feet. It was the doctor who sent
me, but I don't know how well you get along with him,
I mean, I don't have access to that kind of inside information, so I don't know why he said I should come
here, but he did, and so here I am." When I'd finished I
realized it was all a waste of words, but as the head
nurse waited calmly for me to continue, it dawned on
me that I'd left out the most important part, so I
screwed up my courage and stated firmly: "The doctor
says there's a part missing, and wants to put in a piece of

plastic, but I'm against it." Opening a drawer, the head nurse took out a form, scrawled something on it, then signed it, stamped it, and handed it over. It was a detailed document entitled "Permission to Refuse an Operation" with a legal explanation printed on the back. The whole thing was so simple it stopped me in my tracks. "You mean that's all there is to it? I can just give this to the receptionist and go home?" I asked, and when she nodded I turned to go, but the boldness of what I'd done suddenly released all the tension that was bottled up inside me, and as the tears welled up, I wanted to speak to her but couldn't think what to say, so for the time being I just wiped my eyes with my fingertips. When, however, she said, "There's a cold wind today, so you should try not to let it blow straight into your eyes," my sentimental feelings drained away and, straightening up, I asked, in a tone so calm it surprised even me, "What happens when they put plastic in your feet?" She gazed out the window, saying simply "Your way of walking changes," which in its very brevity seemed somehow friendly, as if we'd known each other for years, encouraging me to ask "How does it change?" whereupon she opened the drawer again, handed me a pamphlet entitled "The Heel and Other Cultures: A Socio-medical Study," and then, to show me she had no more time to spare, turned back to her work. That's when I realized what it was that had been floating in the air all this time: it was the smell of lavender. Along with this, I understood that although this talk with the head nurse might be a turning point in my life, to her it was just part of her job, the sooner done with the better. I left the room and walked slowly over to the receptionist's window, where I handed in the form, the woman shaking her head again and giving a heavy sigh. While I was waiting for the bus home, darkness fell, setting the treetops off against the sky like shadow pictures; I looked back at the hospital, searching for the head nurse's window, but with all the lights out it might have been any one of them, so I tried to bring on a sentimental mood by reminding myself that if I were in a traffic accident here no one would mourn, as no one knew what I was doing, but my tears were already dry, and now I couldn't even remember why I'd cried.

Unfortunately, I left the pamphlet the head nurse gave me on the bus, which meant I'd have to go on as I was, ignorant of matters concerning the heel, walking a little strangely but, when people laughed, not really understanding why. When I got home I had no appetite, and since dinner wasn't made I threw myself on the bed without even changing into my nightgown, and must have fallen asleep as soon as I closed my eyes. Perhaps because he was away on business, my husband didn't appear in my dream that night; I was alone in what looked like a factory warehouse, and while I waited there a human figure came silently toward me. Though it was too dark to see the face, I could tell from the scent of lavender that it was the head nurse. I collapsed at her knees and started crying my heart out, but she didn't stroke my hair as I'd hoped she would, launching instead into a long explanation of what locksmiths do, and when I protested, "I'm not cut out for that sort of work. I'd be better at breaking locks than making them," she just laughed and said, "But they break locks, too. If you lose your housekey, a locksmith can open any lock for five bills," adding that they did it by gouging out the keyhole with a screwdriver. When I objected, "But that's not what I want to do. I'd rather be a nurse, like you," she embraced me for the first time, as if these were the words she'd been waiting for, and although it occurred to me as I felt her arms around me that the last thing I wanted to be was a nurse, I stayed there, my cheek pressed against hers, inhaling the fragrance of lavender.

Suddenly she pushed me away and looked at her watch. "You'll be late for school," she scolded.

"I don't want to go to school—it's boring," I said, trying to resist.

"Well, then, I guess we'll have to stop meeting here," she replied, which left me no choice in the matter, since the idea of not seeing her again was unbearable. After I'd promised to go, she took my right foot and, holding it to her chest, began caressing it. She stroked the instep around and around until it grew hot, held my toes in her palm and kissed each one of them, but when the kissing escalated to violent sucking, with her front teeth clacking like castanets, I felt uneasy and tried to pull my foot away but it was terribly weak, lying there, limp as a toy, in her hand, and it crossed my mind that I hadn't the strength to go anywhere now, even if I'd wanted to.

I was scared stiff of waking up that morning, since fewer than five bills on the bedside table would mean I'd parted company with the head nurse even in my dreams, presumably to carry on with my married life as before, but when I looked at the table, all five were there after all. My husband could easily have cut off my funds as punishment for falling on the bed like a drunk the night before without even changing into my nightgown, and I wondered why he kept up his end of the bargain so conscientiously, getting up early every morning just to leave me money, as though paying a prostitute he'd never touched. Perhaps he was watching me through a hole in the wall, noting the stupid look on my face when I picked up the cash every morning, or maybe the whole wall was a two-way mirror, with my room open to view like an aquarium from his side.

It's not in my nature to hunt down people in hiding, or drag what's lost in darkness back into the light, but when I'm cornered and have to make a move, or there's an older woman egging me on, you'd be surprised at the things I can do without batting an eye. Still, I wasn't really sure how determined I was when I wandered into town and headed for the business district, looking for a certain shop. Without having been told what the outside of it would look like I somehow knew; one sometimes has the feeling one's been there before.

The locksmith was a tall fellow in a leather apron whose bony body bent so flexibly and in so many different places as he darted around his tiny store that he seemed to have more than the usual number of joints. "Er, excuse me," I began, intending to wait until he'd turned around and decided how to react to me before going on, but when he saw me he neither spoke nor showed a flicker of interest.

"Er, is it true that locksmiths not only make locks

but break them, too?" I asked.

"Who told you that?"

"The head nurse at the general hospital."

"You'd never catch me at a hospital, letting a perfect stranger look in my ears. Haven't been sick or hurt in the last ten years, thank god, but I'm going to stay away from doctors and policemen if it's the last thing I do."

I had obviously rubbed him up the wrong way. Realizing I'd got off to a bad start, looking for a different angle, I decided to be frank.

"My husband is shut up in his room and won't come out, so I want to break down the door and go in there myself," I said.

"Not much of a man, if you ask me," said the locksmith, shaking his head, "hiding in his room just because his wife yells at him."

"No, it's not that—we didn't have a fight or anything," I pleaded, "—he's shut up in there for no reason and won't come out when I call, so I'm really worried." Deceived by my own playacting, my heart was really into it now, and I might have burst into tears if he'd refused, but, apparently shocked by the pallor of my face, he asked, "Suicide?" which I neither affirmed nor denied.

Seeing that it was serious, the locksmith left the

shop to his apprentice, put his tools into a bag, and came back with me to the house. On the way, he asked me what my husband did, and I told him without thinking, "He's a novelist," at which he nodded, muttering, "I guess guys like that spend a lot of time shut up in their rooms." When we stopped in front of the house, I almost lost my nerve, realizing that, through ignorance and impatience, I could well be ruining a perfectly normal marriage. That lingering sense of a hidden part of life on which the curtain never rose, that hint of joy which always slipped away, out of your grasp, until all the other odds and ends grew into a mountain, filling your days—wasn't this what every couple experienced? And if this was the case, I thought, there was no reason to destroy it; but then, seized with a desire to pry open my husband's room, grab him, and stare him in the face, whether he was a child, an old man, or a corpse, I urged the locksmith on: "Come on, his room's on the second floor."

"The floor in that hall creaks so bad it sounds like it's screaming. Gives you the creeps," the locksmith grumbled as he followed me up the stairs before stopping at the black door, whose color he didn't even comment on, and saying to himself, "Now that's a funny shape for a keyhole," as he stepped back to examine it.

"You mean you can't break it?" I asked, worried already, but he ignored me, picked up his screwdriver, and was kneeling in front of the door like someone praying when he suddenly turned around, looked up at me sharply, and announced, "I charge five for this, you know." I showed him the bills in my pocket, and with a curt nod he set about destroying the keyhole. Since you can't break a "hole" it must have been the lock he was working at, but all I could see was the keyhole changing shape, growing larger and more grotesque, and though it made me sick to watch, I couldn't think of a reason to stop him doing what I'd asked him to start in the first place. Anyone would feel dismayed to see a stranger's tools smashing something they'd thought was all right the way it was, but I simply didn't know what else to do. The work must have been going smoothly, for the locksmith started humming a tune, putting everything he had into gouging out, so to speak, the insides of the hole, until he seemed about to tumble through and into the room on the other side. I watched his fingers, becoming more and more absorbed until the strength went out of my legs, so that when the door creaked open I couldn't move. It was a big, gray room, empty as though someone had just moved out, and though I knew what the little blob lying in the middle of the floor was as soon as I saw it, I gritted my teeth, determined not to translate it into words. I didn't want to acknowledge it, not because it made me sad or angry, but so that something as utterly meaningless, as totally absurd as this should disappear without a trace, and it *would*, too—this whole story would vanish from the world if I could only forget it; before I lost my head and told someone, I had to erase the memory, even if it meant taking drugs to do it. The locksmith didn't know what was going on, so he wouldn't remember, and it wasn't that peculiar, surely, for a dead squid to be found in the middle of a room, nor was there anything particularly strange about my standing here, a widow; so if only I could get rid of all these weird connections and sequences of events, I should be able to make a fresh start, for it wasn't me who'd killed him, I told myself— all I'd done was have the door broken down so I could get my eggs and notebooks back, I repeated silently, over and over again.

THE GOTTHARD RAILWAY

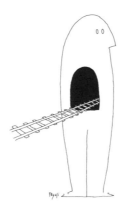

I was offered a chance to ride on the Gotthard Railway once. I've never actually met anyone called Gotthard. "Gott" means "god" and "hard" is, well, hard. It's a very old name, so it may have died out by now. But even though I've never come across one before, about three minutes after I heard the name for the first time, a vivid image formed in my mind. A beard like wires sprouting from the cheeks and chin. Lips the color of blood, quivering constantly but refusing to speak. Eyes like beads about to be smashed, full of fear and anger.

The Swiss talk of the railway "passing through Gotthard." Through a man's body, in other words. The mountain penetrated by this long tunnel is also known as St. Gotthard. Which means that the train runs through a saint's belly. I've never been inside a man. Everyone was once trapped in the belly of a woman we call Mother, and yet we go to our graves without knowing what a father's body is like inside.

The idea of riding through a saint thrilled me, so I accepted immediately. The offer came from the editor of a Zurich newspaper who spoke so politely his syllables might have been ironed. Gotthard is gloomy, oppressive; that's why we want a foreigner to ride on it, to lighten it up a bit, he said on the phone. The only trouble is that I am not the Japanese writer he'd been planning to ask for an article about the tunnel. Nor was it a case of mistaken identity. It was more like deliberate fraud, actually.

I caught the Gotthard bug. It was like the fever children can work up, passionately longing for a summer holiday at some beach they've never seen after hearing the name from their parents. The words "Gotthard Railway," transformed into the color of rusty iron, the cold, hazy April air, and the subtle vibrations of the rails, heard only by lonely passengers sitting by themselves gazing out the window, made my throat sore with longing. So I gargled, and then phoned Reiner. Reiner teaches literature at Kiel University. He's not a full professor yet, but his fortieth birthday is still three months off, so he isn't too worried yet. You sometimes hear drunken journalists in bars say that forty is the age when you get serious about moving up in the world. That means I don't have to make something of myself for another ten years. But even if I wanted to be a success, it couldn't happen, since I don't have a profession.

"I've been asked to ride on the Gotthard Railway. I'm really looking forward to it," I told him. Sounding as though he didn't quite know what to say, he mumbled, "You poor thing. Shutting you up in that long, dark tunnel—the Swiss can be awful sometimes." And then I remembered. To be considered an intellectual in northern Germany, you must yearn for the Italian sunshine. No one can understand the sort of mind that likes wandering into mountains or tunnels and not coming out again. But that doesn't necessarily make you mysterious or interesting, either. Just not accepted as "one of us." Which is fine with me, but Reiner doesn't like it when I say things his friends can't understand. Because if they find me incomprehensible, it means I'm out of reach for him as well.

"Do you know a land where the lemon trees flower?... / With you, my love, I long to go." The lines are from a poem of Goethe's. For him, the word "Italy" conjured up visions of ancient ruins bathed in golden sunlight. He was *burdened* with longing, piled up like oversized trash. It's the duty of intellectuals to pine for Italy. They feel an obligation to drink wine. Neither interests me in the slightest. Pouring alcohol down one's throat isn't worth the trouble. I'd rather crawl into Gotthard's belly and stay there for a while. Lighting my way with a kerosene lamp. Heating up cans of bean soup. In the pitch dark. Living there in the tunnel, where the only time I can see the backs of my hands is when a train comes through. What I want is not the southern sunshine, or a view from the peak, but to lose my sight deep in the mountain. That's why I'm unacceptable to both German intellectuals and Japanese tourists. For to the intellectuals, Gotthard is merely an eyesore that cuts off the sunlight, and the tourists prefer the pristine Jungfrau to the whiskered Gotthard.

At a secondhand bookshop in Zurich, I let the very pleasant owner talk me into buying a novel with an unpleasant title. I don't know how you'd translate it. *Penetrating Gotthard*—something like that. ("Penetration" is a word I don't care for. It has none of the appeal of "cul-de-sac" or "cavern.") The author, Felix Moschelin, is famous in Switzerland but completely unknown outside his own country. There are lots of artists like that in Switzerland, just as there are in Japan. Masters within national boundaries. The volume was too thick to fit in my handbag. Seven hundred and fourteen pages long. While I had no intention of reading it from start to finish, I was sure I'd find passages that appealed to me as I leafed through it. It's good to have books like that on hand.

"This," the man in the bookshop explained, "is a historical novel about the construction of the Gotthard Railway, one hundred and fifty years ago. Moschelin worked through a mountain of reference material to write it. It isn't just a story he made up"—as if he assumed one would be hostile toward something purely imaginative. I took this as an insult to fantasy, feeling I should stick up for it. "It wouldn't make any difference to me if that tunnel were 'made up,'" I said, and saw a stony darkness form in his eyes, low down in them, making him look like a distant relative of Gotthard himself. If you scraped off Gotthard's sharp angles and put a pair of glasses on him, over eyes hungry for the written word, this was the sort of face you might end up with.

In the same shop I bought a map of central Europe. When I opened it up I saw Gotthard in all his majesty lying right across the center. I didn't know he was right in the middle of Europe. But you can never rely on maps for that sort of information. Japanese maps all put Japan in the center, as any other country seems entitled to do for itself if it feels like it.

Gotthard stretched across the map. His fingertips

touched Italy. His left eye was Zurich, Basel the right. Schwyz was his heart. He had mountains around his belly; there, I thought, was where Switzerland was born. Or I almost thought so, before realizing it was an illusion in the dream I had last night. Countries aren't born from mountains. No womb ever held a nation— even one surrounded by water.

Last night in my hotel room in Zurich, I had such a bad dream it woke me up. There were five mountains of paper. Important contracts or something, apparently. They were piled up on a red carpet, and looking at them from above, I could see they formed a cross. When I got closer, I saw that all the documents were blank. As white as snow. Snowy mountains. On the wall next to my bed was a photograph of a snow-covered Andermatt. I noticed it for the first time when I woke up from the dream. People seem to find it comforting to think that mountains are mothers, at the same time believing that they're basically male. This applies to Mt. Fuji. Why do postcards with "Nippon" on the stamps always have a photo of Mt. Fuji bang in the middle of them? As though Fuji were one of Japan's parents, with Mother Nature the other.

"With its head above the clouds / Fuji is the highest mountain in Japan," is the beginning of a song I used to

know. I thought the rest woul.
sang it in bed, but the words "W.
clouds / Here comes King Kong"
behind and swallowing it up. I'd st.
lively, but every time I got to the w.
turned into King Kong.

I reached Zurich's Central Station the 1
way ahead of schedule. The letter had sa.
catch the 9:30 train to Lugano; when I got
Goldau at 9:45, a Mr. Berg, who'd been an eng.
the Gotthard Railway for the past forty years, wo
waiting for me on the platform. I was to board
him, riding in the engineer's cab. Berg had retired
cently, and was now working as a guide for journalists
who came to do a story on the railway.

The train for Lugano was already there, waiting.
There was a Swiss flag on the front of it. Not a cloth
one, of course, but a metal plaque. The train at the next
platform had one, too. A white cross on a red background. How awful it would look if Japanese trains all
had the Rising Sun on the front. You'd get the depressing impression that whole neighborhoods of wartime
children were being evacuated to the countryside. Seeing their flag must be quite different for the Swiss. Perhaps they put it on their trains for good luck, like those

wooden busts of women sticking out of the prows of ships. Or maybe to keep the mountain spirits from causing train wrecks by starting landslides, or suddenly giving the sweet little brooks that flow beside the tracks the power and fury of the sea.

The white cross in the middle of the Swiss flag. Just thinking of its four arms makes European geography, which can easily slide together in a gooey mess if you're not careful, fall neatly into place. Of course, anything that's too orderly is probably a lie. Still, it's comforting when things look methodical. As long as you have a map, you don't mind getting lost. But without one, even when you know where you are you can still be worried sick.

The cross on the Swiss flag is reassuring. Go right and you reach Austria. Go left and you're heading for France. Up is toward Germany, down toward Italy. But does Europe really exist? Or do we just think so because everyone talks as though it did? Or because there are maps of it? I look at my map again. There certainly seems to be a place called Europe. And if there's a Europe, there's no reason why there shouldn't be a Switzerland too. Let's take their word for it. It's safer that way.

As I stared at the Swiss flag, my vision gradually

blurred, and the design began to change. The blood that was supposed to stay frozen outside the cross started to run, seeping slowly into the center. The cross drank it in, and turned into a fat red ball. As it lost its blood, the background grew pale, then finally pure white. Before I knew it, I was looking at the Japanese flag. Until that moment, I'd never noticed how closely the two flags resembled each other: the cross of Christ and the sun of Amaterasu; different shapes, but both islands of a sort, surrounded by the surfaces they lie upon. It's an unusual design, quite different from the common tricolor pattern on the German, French, and Italian flags, for example. Two sacred islands, standing alone. Isolated, yet brash enough to plant themselves in the center of the world before anyone notices.

As soon as I got on the train it started. Off to the right was Lake Zurich. On the map it looks like a long teardrop, falling from the city's eye. But though on paper it's weeping, from the window all one sees is a flat stretch of water, with nothing sad about it.

When I got off the train at Arth-Goldau, a man like a white birch was standing on the platform waiting for me. "I'm Berg. How do you do?" he said.

The ladder to the engineer's position was steeper than the stairway at the back of a factory warehouse.

The cab was like the tiny room at the top of a tower where Dr. Faust was sitting in a play I'd gone to see with Reiner not long before, perched high in the air all by itself. Are engineers tower-dwellers, too, then? This one greeted us, barely moving his thick, soft lips. He set out two wooden chairs for us next to his seat. Though didn't say so, for some reason he seemed pleased to have us sitting beside him. Berg started explaining how fast the train was going. His commentary was my only link with the driver, who said nothing. When he'd been an engineer himself, Berg hadn't talked much either, apparently: "Drivers talk less and less as time goes on." And now talking was his job. I thought his information would bring the world of these silent engineers closer to me. But that was impossible. Their lives aren't made out of words. Mine, on the other hand, is. I would never understand our engineer. But is there anything in this world that *isn't* made out of words?

Underneath the driver's shoe is a pedal like the ones on old-fashioned sewing machines which he keeps his foot on at all times. If for any reason he happens to lose consciousness, the pedal springs up and puts the brakes on automatically. There is no connecting passage to the other cars. Only a telephone. The engineer's cab is totally isolated. The anticipation in the eyes of passengers looking forward to sunny Italy, children's voices singing songs about the forest, the full-color spreads in travel magazines, and the ooh's and aah's coming from the cars with panorama windows are all part of a far-away world. Even so, doesn't it warm his heart just a little to think of all the living, breathing people he's towing? Maybe it's not warmth but responsibility he feels, weighing him down like a heavy load. When he drives freight trains at night, in ten or more cars there's not a living thing in sight. Just tonnage. Alone, with ten loads of silence behind him, he speeds through the darkness, broken only by signal lights.

He was now pulling thirteen cars, weighing a total of six hundred tons, at a speed of 120 kilometers per hour. When we entered a single-track tunnel, I itched with pleasure from my shoulders to my elbows, inside and out. The tunnel was a gullet, and I was its food. The thrill of sliding down a throat. Do the things we eat feel it, too? This was too strange to discuss with Berg. But I ended up telling him anyway. Revealing something you're almost certain won't be understood is a sign of trust. I knew Berg trusted me, because he told me about so many things that didn't make sense to me. "I doubt this will interest you," he would say, "so if it gets boring, tell me and I'll stop," and then launched into a lecture on the history of railroad technology from the steam engine to the most recent models, peppered with words I'd never heard. So, as a token of gratitude, I told him what was on my mind: "This feels like going down someone's throat. It's terrific." But Berg was concerned. "Don't worry, this is the only tunnel with a single track," he explained. "And there's another tunnel right next to this one, for trains going in the opposite direction." He obviously didn't understand, just as I'd expected. I was only trying to tell him how pleased I was. After all, if throats were a double track, we'd be bringing up everything as soon as we had eaten. And that would be pretty uncomfortable. It's enough having a windpipe that's a double track.

"You compare everything to your own body," Reiner had complained the previous Sunday.

"That's right. I feel everything's part of me." We were walking as usual along the promenade at Kiel's harborfront, with the open Baltic Sea beyond. The smell of engine oil spoiled things a bit. There was a wind blowing, carrying the fragrance of yellow flowers.

"So do you think that boat over there's a part of you? What about those containers stacked up over there? Or that stray tabby cat? Or this empty Coke bottle with the top broken off? Come to think of it, they call dimwits 'empty bottles' in a dialect somewhere—where is that?" A seagull flew overhead, screeching like a cat in heat.

"That means you're an empty bottle. Here, let me put my finger in." I stuck a finger into Reiner's ear. And then his mouth. The joints on my finger got sticky, covered with lukewarm saliva. "If I push it all the way down to your esophagus, I bet that'd hurt." My finger slipped in deeper. Reiner coughed violently. Our "Buddha in the throat" is what they call an "Adam's apple."

The train started up a slope. "On an uphill grade, the speed drops to eighty kilometers per hour. For every kilometer, we climb twenty-six meters. Unlike motorcars, trains can't handle steep slopes," Berg explained apologetically. Not that I wanted to climb straight up. Speed didn't interest me either. "Slow is fine with me / I like it that way": I remembered riding in a car once, humming these lines from a popular song.

Nothing else mattered as long as I could stay like this, inside the tube. I'd sometimes wondered what it would be like to slide down an animal's gullet. Would I have to be chewed up first? Couldn't I just be swallowed, all in one piece? It wouldn't have to be all of me—just a bit would do. A finger, for instance. "If I die, cut off my index finger and feed it to your cat." Reiner keeps a black cat. Whenever I go over to visit, it crouches in the corner, never taking its eyes off me. If I get too close, it dashes off somewhere. I've always wanted to be eaten by an animal when I die. But if I talk too much about being eaten, people might think we were cannibals where I come from, so I only mention little things like fingers. Even a Christian surely wouldn't object to something as harmless as feeding an index finger to a cat? But it pays to be careful: there *are* people over here who might start wondering if the Japanese eat human flesh.

Trains store up the energy they produce while they're going downhill, so one engine can go uphill on the energy generated by three going down. Cars are making the world dirtier. Mr. Berg agreed with me on that. I always hit it off with people who don't like cars. "Why don't we wrap them all in a big sheet and dump them in the Baltic?" I suggested, but he just stared at me without cracking a smile. The Swiss aren't familiar with the Baltic, so maybe it didn't register with him.

He then told me about a plan to build a fifty-kilometer tunnel underground, taking a pamphlet out of his bag to show me. The idea was to keep the steady stream of trucks carrying goods between Germany and

Italy out of sight where they couldn't pollute the air and kill Swiss trees, he said.

(Truck drivers race through the darkness. Around the middle of the tunnel, they start thinking, "What if I never get out?... What if my life ends right here? There's no exits or anything along the way. Just have to keep going for another twenty minutes. Feels like I'm going to pass out. This may be it—" Just then, a young man appears in the headlights, standing with his back against the tunnel wall. His white shirt clings to his chest, soaking wet. He's crying, his face buried in his hands. What the hell is he doing here all on his own? The driver slams on the brakes. The front of the truck behind him looms in the rearview mirror, a circle of light. A collision's unavoidable. Hit from the rear, he blacks out. The driver in the truck behind him is killed instantly.)

I don't understand how truck drivers feel about their work. Frankly, it wouldn't bother me if trucks vanished off the face of the earth. If things must be transported, ships and trains can do the job. They say trucks save money, but it's the company that profits, not the drivers; more work wouldn't benefit them at all. But that's just my opinion. As I said before, I have no idea how they feel about it. Never having worked for a living, I know next to nothing about working people. I've written other people's Master's theses, penned anonymous pornographic novels, delivered what looked like German-made stuffed animals to Moscow, taken care of pedigree dogs during vacations, and copied rental videos, earning my bread from jobs that verge on fraud. The words "an honest day's work" sound as nasty to me as a pair of rusty scissors.

A very busy Japanese writer living in Germany asked me to go on this trip as a proxy. "But won't they know?" I said. "Don't worry," I was told, "anyone from the newspaper who comes to your hotel in Zurich will only have talked to me on the phone, and even if they've seen my picture somewhere, all Japanese faces look alike to them, so there's nothing to worry about." I was told to ride the train, take notes, and tell her about it when I got back. That was all there was to it. Nothing was said about what exactly I was supposed to report.

Officially, I'm working for a Japanese computer company run by someone Reiner knows. They don't actually have enough money to hire anyone, but since there was no other company in Kiel I could ask to sponsor me, and getting a visa would be difficult without a job, I'm posing as their employee. Sometimes I go to the area they're in and sit on a bench in the park in front of the building, eat a sandwich, and then go home. For me, this is going to work. When most of what you do is a bit of a fraud, the word "profession" starts to look like the Berlin Wall. That's gone now, of course, but my wall is safe and sound. I can almost touch it. The surface of the word "profession" is hard and rough, the inside mixed with poison. It's this that prevents me crossing over. And what is there on the other side? Only what people longingly refer to as "the other side."

There's nothing quite so flat as the surface of a lake. Just looking at the one we were passing made me feel dazed. Apparently, the people who lived around the Urnersee were a bit flat themselves. I could barely see the stone monument to Schiller, inscribed in gold, on the opposite shore. It appeared to be standing in the water. But I wasn't sure; perhaps it was on land. "This is where the famous legend of William Tell, the subject of Schiller's play, came from," said Mr. Berg. Under pressure from a Hapsburg magistrate, we're told, a hunter from a village in the canton of Uri was forced to shoot an apple off his own son's head. His arrow split the apple clean in half, and he went on to win the freedom of his commune. But the original legend has a very different slant to it. That's what Schiller rubbed out. "Schiller's books should all be wrapped in a sheet and dumped in the Baltic," I once said to Reiner. He looked up, startled, as if it was his name I'd mentioned. There was fear in his eyes. He then scooped a bit of apple sauce onto his fork and pushed it between his thin lips as though it tasted awful. Apple sauce is always served there with thin slices of boiled beef, so it wasn't my fault. I didn't force him to eat it—the apple, that is.

William Tell must have wanted, basically, to kill his son. If not, he couldn't possibly have put an apple on the boy's head and shot it off that way. It wouldn't matter how much pressure he was under. When people say they were forced to do something, it's usually an excuse. Oedipus claimed fate made him sleep with his mother, but there were rumors that subconsciously he'd wanted it all along. Just as William Tell subconsciously was hoping his son would die.

Speaking of apples: the apple is that dubious fruit Christians say the serpent offered to Eve, who then fed it to Adam, which started people indulging in what's known as sex. So shooting one off your son's head could be taken to mean purging his body of the seed of pleasure he'd received from Woman. That's what I'll tell Reiner when I get back to Kiel. Either the child or sex—one of them had to be shot down, eradicated. Which would you have chosen? If you think they're both just things that happen inside women, you're wrong. I want to take at least one of Schiller's books, wrap it in a sheet soaked in apple juice, and dump it in the Baltic. And I want you to stop munching apples in bed every morning.

The train entered a rotary tunnel. We had to go through a number of these before reaching the long Gotthard Tunnel. The train would make one complete revolution inside the mountain, and come out in roughly the same place. It had to make up for its inability to climb steep slopes in distance, circling gradually higher. You could see how the track curved from the engineer's seat. Otherwise, you probably wouldn't have noticed any change there in the dark. People's sense of direction is hopeless. The white cross on the Swiss flag spun around in my head like a windmill. Every time we came out of a tunnel I could see Wassen Cathedral on the opposite side of the tracks, switching from right to left and then back again. If it weren't for that, I probably wouldn't have bothered to wonder what was going on. That's funny, I thought: I'm being turned. But do people actually *say* that? It sounds like a way of saying you're being swindled. Yes, I could swear something I can't see is turning me 360 degrees. But people say they're being "taken," not "turned." We're all being taken for a ride up Gotthard on this train, slowly up and up. Take, or turn? Anyway, it's so dark here that I can't complain about being turned.

I remember turning Reiner around on the beach once. He was lying on his back, so I just grabbed one of his ankles and spun him around. As his body moved, creaking like the gears of a rusty machine, it sank a little further into the sand. His bottom was the axis; his eyes were shut tight but smiling. With his swimming trunks twisted out of shape, he slowly disappeared in the hot sand, to the sound of a distant motorbike drawing nearer, wheezing all the way. When I finally let his foot go, I could hardly see him at all. Only his penis was left sticking out, like Faust's tower in the land of the Lilliputians.

"I remember once a calf got separated from the herd and was standing on the tracks," Berg said to me. "I felt bad about it. Because by the time you actually see something in front of you, it's too late. Even if you slam on the brakes, the train doesn't stop right away. I hit two people, too. There are still quite a few railway suicides. The average number killed by a driver in a forty-year period is two. Sometimes they don't bleed at all. It just feels like slamming into a big sack of grain. Animal or human, bodies all make the same sound, a thud. But the impact isn't always enough to break the skin. It's a tough surface, skin. Makes you hope maybe this one will be all right. But it never is. Even if there's no blood and you can't see any bones sticking out, their insides are a mess. So smashed up you can't mend them—link them up, plug them, glue them or stitch them back together again."

The train slipped into the V between two sheer cliffs that rose on either side. The surface of the rock was charred black with smooth patches, raw as though the skin had been torn off. A few miserable weeds clung to the rock walls like hair the razor has missed. GÖSCHENEN: a town built when the tunnel was under construction. The travel guides say it's the ugliest town in Switzerland. And that the name is grating enough to suit it. Göschenen. Like a reminder of some disaster, a shadow steeped in blood seems to weigh down on the shoulders of this town caught between two walls of rock, where the air contains compounds so dense you can't say what color they are. "I'm getting off here," I told Mr. Berg. His shoulders jerked up. He must have thought I was frightened, and did his best to reassure me. "But accidents in the tunnel are so rare you could almost say they never happen. Everything is thoroughly checked. Nearly every day we walk around in pairs to make sure everything's in order, that nothing has fallen on the tracks."

But what could there possibly be on the tracks? A dragon's eye dropped out of its socket? A spike heel from a woman's shoe? I wasn't scared, I just wanted to stay there a while. At the end of the platform yawned Gotthard's black mouth. I abandoned the idea of getting off. I didn't have the courage to tell Berg that something about this place appealed to me. With the darkness looming ahead, the words connecting us were gone.

There was hardly any light in the engineer's cab. If the rest of the train was this dark, the passengers would be clutching their wallets to their chests, waiting for the exit to the tunnel with faces like soda water. The darkness was soft as velvet, and smelled slightly of tobacco. I like it without any light—with the darkness pushing in gently from all sides. "The tunnel is fifteen kilometers long, so we'll be out in about ten minutes," Berg said, and then fell silent. My eyes were becoming accustomed to the gloom. At one point there was an open space in the tunnel wall, like an alcove or a small shrine. Dimly, I could see a small statue of the Virgin Mary.

But no, it couldn't be, that couldn't be the Virgin standing there, I thought as the train began to slow down, finally stopping altogether like a listless swing. I looked at the engineer's face, but it was too dark to see his expression. He stood motionless, as if frozen bolt upright. I moved closer, bringing my mouth near his cheek. A wax doll. "Is something wrong?" No answer. I turned to Mr. Berg. He was standing, too. Like a white birch. Its bark kept my words away. The thing glowed vaguely in the darkness before us. The muscles in my shortsighted eyes expanded and contracted, wanting and then not wanting to see.

Still glowing, it came nearer. Broad shoulders and extremely short legs. The whole body shone white. Then it disappeared.

The driver bent forward. Berg cleared his throat. The layer of ice that seemed to have held the train frozen in place melted, and as the cars warmed up, we began to move slowly down the track. We heard the sounds of machinery again. We'd been in a silent world. "What was that just now?" No one answered. Had I really asked? Apparently not. Perhaps our minds had been frozen for a while as well.

Before we came out of the tunnel, I saw two balls of light ahead. Then we hit one head-on. I leaned out the window and looked back to see that it had now turned black. AIROLO. The two "O's" looked like the twin exits of the tunnel we'd just emerged from. That must be it: as a reminder of the Gotthard Tunnel, or even a substitute for it, its shape was carved into the name of the place. Airolo, designed to open a bright, cheery hole in you every time you said the word. All together now, "Airolo!" We were now in the Italian-speaking region of Switzerland. And there were more of these mementos—in every town, in fact. Why else would each have its own pair of open "O's"? LAVORGO, GIORNICO, BODIO, and when passengers reach the junction at Bellinzona, they can choose between two more: COMO or LOCARNO. My head was filled with Gotthard. No matter where I went, all I saw was the twin "O's" embedded in the names of places. The tunnel was saying, "Come back." The exit wanted to turn into an entrance. The womb was calling, "Come back!"

"I'm going back to Göschenen," I said, deciding to be honest about it, and noticing the little wound this made in Berg's eye. I've often seen the same thing happen with Reiner. There are, admittedly, some things that simply must be said, even if it means turning your heart into cold steel, but when you grit your teeth and say them, you see this wounded look. I could have lied and pretended to go on to Como, gaily waving out the window, then quietly getting off at the next station to catch the train back. That way, I would have saved Berg a lot of worry. For Como is a beautiful place, one anybody would want to see. But why do I always have to be the one who lies? The lying I do on the job is quite enough. I was going to Göschenen. To the ugliest town in Switzerland. Everyone else might think of it that way, but I didn't. So goodbye. Which may have been as cruel as telling Reiner I didn't want to drink wine or go to Italy.

In Göschenen I saw neither people nor any signs of human activity, only the marks left where the snow had begun to melt, blotches in the landscape that made me feel miserable. Don't make me look at this, I thought: it reminds me of those boys I'm always seeing around Kiel Station with their heads shaved down to the raw skin in patches, as if to punish themselves. Or is it a protest, to show their parents? To say, "There are the scars where you hit me," to their fathers, or "These are the marks you left when you licked me dry" to their mothers. The tufts of brown hair the clippers have missed look dirty, pitiful. Like Gotthard himself. They shaved the mountain, drilled a hole in it, tortured it. Raised their pickaxes cheerfully, as if playing the cymbals in a brass band. Opening Moschelin's novel at random, I scanned the pages, my toes growing cold as I read.

> Listen, all of you! It is time the people were heard! All this frenzy about building a tunnel is becoming more than we can tolerate. Switzerland is a free nation. We do not need a Railroad King. And this one is more unsavory even than the bureaucrats, or the knights of Austria, or the army from Burgundy, and more of a menace than any high-toned aristocrats, or Napoleon's marauders, or a band of old warlords clashing their Prussian swords together. We must drive them back, these serpents that slither their way into the bosom of Helvetia!

I can understand why they didn't want a tunnel. It's been a century and a half since it happened, but I'm sure I would have felt the same way. Foreign capital and Italian sunshine—who needs them? All I want is to hide in the darkness of Gotthard, without blasting holes in it or hauling in steel. Does that make me an isolationist?

Are the serpents trains, their bellies lined with golden scales shining in the sunlight? Or do all those eyes honing in on the mountain, obsessed with tunneling, look like snakes when they finally break through it?

I, too, am a serpent. But I'm not interested
breasts, in worming my way into the firm layer of
that covers Helvetia's. A man's soft belly is more to
taste, a mound of flesh fed on fetuses that forgot
be born, decaying, in a dream. Digging inch by in
through hard rock doesn't appeal to me. I want som
thing soft enough to melt into.

> One knows there are people of gentle outlook wh
> are content with nothing more than peace an
> quiet. But we are a wild and restless race; we thriv
> on the din of exploding dynamite. Let others plant
> the corn and harvest the grapes. We have chosen
> to pit ourselves against hard rock. And if it should
> refuse to yield to us, we shall rejoice in the oppor-
> tunity this provides to show how much stronger
> our will is than its own!

The room at my hotel in Göschenen was long and
narrow. Unlike the sad, scarred, gray and black stone
outside, its walls were a soft yellow, the color of cus-
tard, food that's comforting when you have a cold. I
sprawled out on the bed to read the Moschelin book. It
wasn't time to roll over on my back yet. The shadows
were growing longer in the afternoon sun: too early for
bed, too late to go outside. Not really, though, that was

just an excuse. I wanted to stay here, surrounded by these four walls. Wherever I am, when I close my eyes, I feel I'm in a tunnel. And, wherever it leads, the direction I'm facing is always forward. Which means the entrance to the tunnel is always at the back of my head. If I try to look back at it, what's behind me moves too, remaining out of sight. I shut my eyes and think of the entrance in its fixed position, and start turning in the tunnel. I open my eyes to find myself in the same place. I close them again. The tunnel appears. I revolve. Behind is still back there, receding further and further away.

Reiner's getting fat around the middle. When I press his belly button with my finger, it just keeps on going in. There must be a bone somewhere, I say to myself. But I can't feel anything. I get worried and stop. "This is the finger you wanted my cat to have, isn't it?" says Reiner, grabbing it roughly. "Ouch!" I yell automatically. My finger is all bone, with only a thin layer of flesh over it. Just a little squeeze and it hurts. So if it went all the way into his stomach, it might get stuck in the folds of fat and break off. In fat as white as snow. And marbled meat, too, meets its maker. I want to get inside your belly.

The rock could be willing, showing consideration

and good nature. It could also be cruel, and white as marble tombstones. Or black as children's slates. At times it was soft as the dough Mother kneads for bread, at others hard as the whetstone Father uses to sharpen knives.

When dusk fell, I was still in the hotel, flipping through the pages of the book; probably a dangerous mood coming on, but not up to doing anything about it. Go out and talk to someone if you think you're going crazy shut up indoors like this, I told myself. But I like being cooped up. That's how I spend my happiest moments. In hotel rooms. Or train compartments. A tunnel's good, too. I like being confined. Go outside, go out and talk to people; use words that smell like a newspaper fresh from the printing press.

From Göschenen Station, I took the mountain train to Andermatt. I was the only passenger. On the map, Andermatt looks as though it's perched on top of the tunnel. So perhaps there was a hole somewhere leading straight down into it. If I could find it, I might try to get into the tunnel from above. Or at least peer down into it. Buying my ticket was like getting a chocolate bar in a movie theater: that sense of expectation, hearing the silver paper crackle as you peel it off. The train started moving at a snail's pace. Like a ride through the Haunted House in an amusement park, it made a terrible racket, deliberately clattering down the track, swaying too far back and forth as it crept along the narrowest ledge possible, so that it seemed about to fall off at any moment. Outside was a mountain pass that looked like a stage setting. With a knight riding through it on horseback, it would have been perfect for a scene in a historical movie. And then, quite suddenly, it was snowing. I'd hardly been on the train ten minutes when spring vanished and I entered a world wrapped in silver paper. Snowflakes flew by like the tiny stars that sparkle across the screen of an old film, and you couldn't help smiling. The snow was piled deep on the roads. For no particular reason, a station attendant we passed had a muddled-looking grin on his face. What is it about snow that has this effect on people? Compared to this radiance, spring in Airolo in all its glory would be like a memory of an awful holiday, where the sun beat down without a moment's rest. Snow gave the mountain an air of white wisdom. And I, too, was smiling for no reason when I set out on foot. A huge, empty plain lay surrounded on all four sides by sheer slopes. The shower of light continued to fall on its pristine surface. I was alone there. No one else knew where I was. Within minutes, the snow would erase my footsteps, turning the plain back into a blank page, so I myself might almost not have been there. ("Now that you mention it, there was an Asian woman on the train. She didn't have any ski equipment. Or anything else, for that matter— makes you wonder why she came in the first place." This is what the station attendant might tell the police if they questioned him. I hadn't left an address at the hotel in Göschenen. It might take them a while to work out who I was.) I found myself imagining having an accident. But then the snowfall stopped, and with it my daydream vanished. For right in the middle of this expanse of white, I saw a sign that stopped me in my tracks. NO WALKING HERE. It was incredible! People will try to ban anything. Who in their right mind would put up a sign like that in an empty field? Perhaps they couldn't think of anything else to ban. What other reason could there be? I was sure I'd find other signs as I went along. Like, NO USING TYPEWRITERS HERE. Or, SENTENCES WITHOUT SUBJECTS ARE FORBIDDEN. It was just officialdom making sure people didn't think they could do as they liked out here in the snow.

In front of me, off to one side, was an open pit about a meter across. I wondered if someone had actually dug a hole to look down into the tunnel. I went right over to it. Filled with anticipation, my lungs felt as if they were being tickled inside, which made it hard to breathe. I wheezed with laughter as I stepped forward. Then abruptly I stopped. The hole was deep. Beneath a layer of snow about two meters thick was a black hollow with dark green water flowing slowly along the bottom of it. I was standing on top of a river or lake. So that's why they put the sign up: to keep people from falling in when the snow melted. My knees slipped out of joint and froze that way, making it impossible to move. My mind had already begun to fall, the gap between the frozen surface and the water below pulling me down toward it. Go back the way you came and you'll be OK, I said to encourage myself, and turned around. And what's so bad about dropping down into the darkness of Gotthard anyway? That's where you wanted to go, isn't it? I heard someone laugh. There was nobody around. Perhaps a trace of some distant skier's voice had been caught in the recent snowstorm, and the wind had carried it here. What if this were the last human sound I was to hear? My first step was so tiny and crooked it looked like a joke. Why couldn't I walk straight? The assumption that straight ahead is the shortest way to go doesn't hold up in snow.

The night before Reiner's liver operation, I had a dream. His moist, red-black belly, exposed to view, was filled with penises—like a selection of neatly packaged salamis. "With this many stored away, you've nothing to worry about," a nurse said reassuringly. The surgeon grimly stuck a Japanese doll in among those serried penises, which were all about the same size as it. Jet-black hair. Glazed-looking eyes. I was worried he might leave her there when he sewed Reiner up. But, not knowing the medical term for "a Japanese doll," I couldn't protest.

That sheet of snow was frightening in its whiteness. I wanted to be somewhere rocky—back in Göschenen —a name that itself was made of stone. A name harsh on the ear. One that no human sensibility had shaped according to its taste, whether good or bad. Just stone become a word. GÖ: hard rocks grinding together. SCHE: gravel sliding down the slope to become NEN: the moist clay at the bottom of the valley. Saying the word out loud helped calm me down, and brought some strength back to my knees.

The snow sucked everything into it, even light. There was nothing above it, nothing below. And con-fronting it, I too went blank. Some faint impression of letters written in pencil will always remain however carefully you erase them. But I disappeared completely, like a picture on a screen, leaving nothing behind. It was only by chanting that stone word—Göschenen—that I could hope to find some trace of my lost self, and find my way home. Chanting, I walked on, until at last I saw the station.

> Some of the rock was soft enough to write with, like chalk; some so hard one could have used it to cut glass. There were colors bright and dark. They dug through gray tinged with blue, and a purple shade of brown, with lots of bluish and greenish colors next, then brown, and more green, followed by bright lemon yellow and dull ocher, and the muddy hue of decaying earth, before finding bluish gray again. They saw streaks that looked like lightning, bronze turned green, cylinders of bluish purple, stones black as coal or as beautiful as pomegranates, silver quartz crossed with black lines, rivers of solid pink, and patches of iron against a green background. Through all these shades of color, two teams dug inward from north and south toward the center, where both would find the same color.

There, right in the heart of the mountain, two pick-axes clinked together.

When I got back to the hotel, I lay down on the bed and started leafing through the heavy book again. I read about Italian workers and their shovels; about men who went on digging for ten years, while others quit and found new jobs. And about men who died. The stone did all the talking while the workers dug in silence.

Unable to sleep that night, I went for a walk down to the station. There was no one there. Not even a watchman. A group of bicycles still wrapped in plastic sheets were parked outside like a herd of calves. Perhaps the ghosts of calves killed in railway accidents sneaked out at night to gather by the station for a chat. Come spring, the bikes would probably be rented out to tourists. They had bells on the handlebars like the bells they hang on cows' necks; but these were stone-cold, refusing to shine. Nighttime in the valley, hushed and still. The last train had left long before. I climbed up onto the platform. I couldn't keep my eyes off the mouth of the tunnel. Inside, it was even blacker than the night around me in this valley town. A darkness so deep it wouldn't even let me see myself going in there. Had I really been inside the tunnel? In Gotthard's belly, focus of my dreams? No, I couldn't believe it. I couldn't believe it had ever happened.